HUNTING THE HAUNTING

Joann Reneé Muszynski

Dragonpoe Publishing
Indian Harbour Beach, FL

Book & cover design by Technospider Services
www.technospider.com

Chapter art reprinted within through the generous permission of Friends of West Norwood Cemetery

First trade paperback edition: May 2009

Printed in the United States of America

ISBN - 978-0-578-02389-2

Contact the author:
joann@technospider.com
www.huntingthehaunting.com

To my family, for all their love and support while creating this story, I thank you for all you've given me in the ways of love, critique, help with research, and just for being here.

And to all those who believe that there is more to our world than simple life and death, may you keep on investigating, asking questions and never give up on finding the answers.

Chapter 1

Sarah could not believe she was standing in the middle of an old cemetery on a sunny September day. With her Gucci sunglasses pushed up high on her nose, she looked around with a weary expression on her face.

How old was this cemetery anyway? The grave markers, all chipped and faded, went on forever dotting an ocean of dull green grass. Unmown and forgotten, the grass reached upward grabbing at the stones trying to pull them down into the hidden depths of the earth. The very air was stale, as if she breathed in the exhalations of the dead beneath her feet.

Sarah tilted her head back, gazing up into the sky. The sun sat low, fat and lazy on the horizon. Ribbons of gold, pink, orange and palest blue stretched across the endless sky. Her gaze fell from the pristine heavens and with a sigh she found her friends.

They stood in a semicircle with professional Nikon cameras obscuring their faces. For a moment, Sarah envisioned herself standing before a ring of aliens, their Cyclopean eyes caught the sun and ignited quick sparks of lightning. She listened as their insectile voices whirred, buzzed and chattered as frame after frame of pictures were taken.

She watched her best friend, Jamie, as her short plump body moved backward, Cyclops eye pointed to the ground. Click-snap-click whispered her camera. Sarah sighed again. Clearly she didn't belong here. But when Jamie begged, she always gave in. Jamie swore that something great was going to happen today. Even though Sarah wasn't officially part of the Specters team, Jamie had pleaded. Her ghost-hunting buddies were so wrapped up in their work that she was certain they had forgotten she was even there. Besides not being an official member, she didn't even believe in ghosts. Ha! What a childish fantasy.

"Do you see anything?" Jamie asked.

"No. What am I suppose to see?" she said, looking at Jamie over the rim of her sunglasses.

"Anything. Though usually nothing shows up until after we develop the film," Jamie said.

"Then what's the point of asking if I see anything?" God, she was bored. It felt like they had been there for hours already.

Shane Longley, self-proclaimed founder of their little group called the Specters, stepped forward. His shadow fell over her, blocking the warm sun. He looked her square in the eye.

"We feel for signs, cold spots, eerie sensations, et cetera," he said. "You wouldn't understand. Your mind isn't open enough."

Sarah stood tall and defiant, ready to battle wits with either of them. Her eyes shifted from Jamie's pudgy, child like face to Shane, whose only flaw to his handsome, hard-bodied physique was his incredible arrogance.

"Uh, excuse me," Sarah said. "If I wasn't open minded I wouldn't be standing here, would I? I just don't get what you think you'll find."

"Proof that ghosts are real," Shane said. "And that when a person dies their spirit is often locked here in the mortal world." He mocked her.

Anger writhed along her nerves; if he came just a few feet closer she'd slap him.

"They're real, Sarah," Jamie said. "I know you don't believe now, but just wait and see. Trust me." Jamie pulled at her, dragging her away from Shane.

They moved deeper into the cemetery. Dennis, Todd and Kate huddled together against an enormous tower of blue veined marble. Something there had grabbed their full attention. Dennis' freckled face beamed with excitement while Todd and Kate ran their hands over the stone. Dennis beckoned them to come closer, his smile inviting.

"Can you feel it?" Dennis asked.

"I know I do," Kate said, pressing her heart shaped face against the stone. Pale skin blended against pale stone beautifully. She closed her eyes, breathing in deep then letting it out slowly. "Oh, I definitely feel it!"

All at once, Nikons sprung into action. The Specters turned in small, slow circles clicking away. Shane sprinted over to them and fired his camera. They shot the monument, the ground and the sky. Every angle and every height was taken advantage of. They left no blade of grass untouched, no twig, broken or whole, wanting. From the lens the entire cemetery became spotlighted, an encore demanding praise.

Sarah watched over them with dumbfounded disbelief. How in love they were with the excitement, the energy of whatever it was that they felt there by that statue. Her eyes rolled skyward. She didn't see anything, she sure didn't feel anything and she didn't even have a camera to at least pretend. She crossed her arms over her chest and busied herself by kicking a twig around.

Finally, the Specters called it a wrap and they all piled into Kate's Chevy conversion van.

"I think that went rather well," Shane said, smiling. His eyes fell on Sarah and he offered her a wry little grin.

Giving him a sour look, she focused her attention out the window. A very cold, intense feeling encompassed her, making the hairs on her arms stand on end. Looking back, she could have sworn there was someone standing beside that marble monument. She turned her head away. Invisible fingers crept up along her neck. She shivered.

She struggled to rid herself of the nagging feeling of ghostly hands playing with her. They touched her neck, ran down her spine, pulled at individual strands of hair. They molested her from head to toe and no amount of distance put a stop to it.

"You okay there, Sarah?" Shane asked. Oh how wicked he could be. His eyes shone sharp. He toyed with her, knowing she felt something.

"Just fine," she answered. Why was he bent on aggravating her today?

Once they had reached Jamie's Tudor style home they piled out and ran straight for the dark room at the back of the house. There, they worked in silence. Each absorbed in their own little worlds of creation. When at last they emerged, smelling like photo-processing chemicals, the fruits of their labor yielded a hefty stack of 5x7 inch black and whites.

"What do I look for again?" Sarah asked. The cemetery had held no interest for her, but the photographs opened themselves to her like wordless novels.

"Anything unusual like orbs, lights, shadows, anything that looks out of place," Jamie told her.

"Just keep an open mind," Shane added.

Sarah gave him a dark look but kept her mouth shut.

"We're not crazy," Jamie said with a frown.

"I didn't say a word!" Sarah said.

"You didn't need to," Kate said. "We can see it written on your face."

"Oh come off it!" Sarah said. "What's the big flipping deal? I don't believe in ghosts. You really expect ghosts to just pose and say, 'Hey look at me'? Leave me alone." Hot anger flushed her cheeks. Sarah grabbed a handful of pictures and began scrutinizing them. At least the photos didn't judge her.

Even though she had been there, she had not seen the cemetery the way the camera had been able to capture it. The grass shone bright with tiny flecks of white scattered along the length of each blade, and the sky wrapped itself around the graves. Even the headstones came to life, their gray marble faces engraved with names and dates. As Sarah gave her full attention to one specific shot of the marble monument, her eyes grew wide.

"Oh my God!" she cried out.

How could this be possible?

Chapter 2

"Oh wow, oh wow, oh wow," Jamie chanted, her nose nearly touching the photograph as she examined it closely.

The white stone monument seemed to be illuminated from within, with a white light that formed a ring around it; a ring that spread itself out to fill the entire print. And there was more.

A young woman stood there, her white gown billowing out around her, dark hair waving its way to her shoulders.

"You can see right through her," Kate whispered.

The rest of the cemetery stretched on behind the mysterious woman as she stood slightly behind the stone. She had been so close that any one of them could have moved right through her.

"Oh, this is good," Jamie said. "I can't believe what I'm seeing but there she is!"

"Maybe there's more," Dennis said, riffling through the photos so eagerly that they cascaded off the table.

Getting down on hands and knees, they sorted through the rest of the photographs and found five additional pictures of the woman. Each was slightly different, but the basic shot was the same; the monument, the woman and the sky and grass beyond. It was the woman who changed in each photo. In one, she just stood there, her eyes forward. Then in the next her hand stretched outward as if beckoning to someone. The third revealed her palm turned up, her body turned just enough so that she faced someone.

"Hey, weren't you standing there, Sarah?" Todd asked.

"I don't think so," Sarah said. But those ghostly fingers had returned to run a path up and down the back of her neck.

The fourth picture was quite disturbing. The lady's face was no longer somber. In this shot her face twisted into a mask of worry, her small mouth a perfect O. They pondered this photo for some time until the next event nearly had Sarah running out of the house.

Sarah yelped throwing a photo down onto the table. Her hand flew to her mouth. Jamie took the photo and released her own little yelp. With trembling fingers she offered it to whoever was willing to take it.

The woman had fallen to her knees. A dark shadow hovered above her. Her face, now upturned, was a complete still life of utter fear. What could have driven this woman to such terror?

Sarah couldn't breathe. A ton of bricks sat on her chest, and her rib cage threatened to cave in. She didn't believe in ghosts! They weren't real. They were fantasies. And yet there she was. As clear as can be, her pale dress a shade of bone while her dark eyes shone bright in her blurry face. And that look of terror!

Was it a prank? Was it a trick that Shane had played to throw her off? No. It couldn't be. She had been in the dark room with them. She witnessed every step in the process of developing the film.

"I think I owe you guys an apology," she said hesitantly.

"Now you have to believe," Jamie said throwing her arms around Sarah.

Sarah couldn't meet Shane's eyes. She had made her apology. That was enough. Besides, she was having a hard time taking all this in.

"Well, Miss Nonbeliever," Shane said. "I think you were a medium this afternoon."

He gave her a winsome smile, so perfect upon his perfect face. She could see why he awed all the girls in school. Even though his mouth smiled, his eyes held mystery and wisdom. His golden hair magnified the intense blue of those eyes. He sat back, running a hand through his sun-kissed hair and smiled. Really smiled. He kept his eyes on her.

"Why do you say that?" Sarah asked.

"Look for yourself," he told her. "This ghost was trying to connect with you. She's pointing at you."

Shane arranged the photos in a circle. "Look," he said. "Dennis, Todd and Kate were standing here. I was over here and Jamie had her back to you. And there you are, Sarah. And there's the ghost. It's clear that she was trying to get your attention."

"I don't want to hear this," Sarah told him.

"You're creeping her out, Shane," Kate said, "Knock it off."

But Sarah had heard enough to terrify her.

Was she really a medium?

No, it wasn't possible.

Or was it?

Chapter 3

It was quite late when Sarah decided to go home. Shane offered to drive her since he lived only a few miles further south of her along the same road. Her first impulse, given what had happened, was to reject his offer. But she couldn't bring herself to do that even if he was the last person she wanted to be left alone with.

Shane's Mazda RX-8 purred quietly as they drove through the starless, silent night, leaving the town and its lights behind them. Sarah was too tired to say much and Shane seemed lost in his own thoughts. When he finally spoke, she jumped.

"Sorry," he laughed. "I was just going to ask if you were all right."

"I'm fine, just tired," she said. "Turn here."

"There's no light on," Shane said, pulling into the driveway.

"Nope. My mom works late most of the time. She's horrible at remembering to leave a light on," she said.

"You're going to be okay alone?" he asked.

"I usually am," Sarah said. "Thanks for the ride."

The truth was, she didn't think she *would* be okay. The darkness seemed to swallow up the little house. And the nearest neighbor was half a mile away and at the back stretched thick, dark woods. She dreaded the moment that Shane would pull away and take the headlights' halogen glow with him.

"Hey," Shane said. "Listen. No hard feelings about today, okay? I know what the rest of the school thinks about me. I've gotten used to it. It's hard, being thrown into this so fast. I know it was for me."

Sarah gave him a puzzled look, not at all certain what he meant.

"Never mind," he said. "The point is that I was on the defensive side earlier. I had no right being so rude to you. Friends?"

Sarah smiled. "Well, I wasn't exactly an angel myself. Good night, Shane. Thanks for the ride home."

Standing by the front porch, she waved as Shane backed out onto the street. She continued to stand there until the two red eyes of his taillights disappeared around the bend. Reluctantly, she let herself into the empty house to be greeted by her cat, Frisko, who offered a hello by rubbing his head against her leg.

"Hello, kitty," she said.

Going to the kitchen, she opened a can of tuna flavored cat food, fed the cat and heated herself some soup. Too tired to eat much, she wasted no time getting into bed.

All she wanted to do was close her eyes and wipe out the entire day. She wanted to forget it all; the cemetery and especially the photo she could neither explain nor deny.

Sarah pulled the lilac and green comforter up to her chin. Listening to the frogs and crickets outside chirping, she allowed her body to relax. She concentrated on the rustling trees out back. They were outside and she was safe in her room. She closed her eyes.

BANG!

Sarah bolted upright, clutching the blankets in her hands.

"Mom?" she called out. "Is that you?"

BANG!

Sarah was on her feet in an instant and grabbed her father's baseball bat, which she kept. It was the one thing he had left her before vanishing one stormy summer night a little over a year ago.

Very carefully, she opened the door and peeked around the corner. Walking on tiptoe, she inched her way down the hall towards the living room where she thought the noise had come from, seeing nothing but deep puddles of inky shadow pooling on the floor in front of the locked windows. Heart pounding, she watched for any sign of movement.

Crassshhhhhh! The sound of glass breaking reverberated along the walls.

"Emily!" yelled a voice ripe with anger.

Sarah didn't move. Her mind raced as she went over all the

things her mother had taught her to do in case something like this should ever happen. Get the phone, have your baseball bat ready, lock yourself in your room, call 911. Okay, she had her bat. Now all she needed was the phone, which was in the kitchen! How stupid! What good was a cordless phone if you left it on the other side of the house?

"Emily if you don't get out here, I swear I will kill you!"

Maybe it was time to go back to her room and lock the door. His voice was like thunder, rattling her nerves.

However, since she wasn't Emily, perhaps the intruder would realize he had the wrong house and go away. In any case, she had to be better off behind a locked door than out in the hallway.

But as soon as she turned to run back to her room, a rush of frigid air slammed against her. She stumbled and fell to the floor, dropping the bat in the process. She watched in horror as it rolled away.

"Emily!" This time he sounded as though he was standing over her. She couldn't see anything but dark shadows looming along the wall.

Sarah threw her hands up over her head. *Oh god, I'm going to die!* she thought.

She felt a heavy weight, like a booted foot, pressing against her back, her stomach pressed hard into the cold tile.

"I told you before that I don't like it when you play games." Whoever he was, he spat out the words.

"I – I'm not Emily," Sarah told him.

Instantly the weight was removed from her back and the bitter coldness was gone. Sarah sat up. The strange man was nowhere to be seen, but she could see a faint and wavering light. An orb floated in the air just a few feet from her face. As it advanced slowly, Sarah scooted backwards on her butt, trying to keep whatever it was from reaching her.

Still it came closer and closer until she could clearly see that it was a face. She realized that it was the woman from the cemetery and that her eyes were brimming with tears.

"Help me," she cried out, flying towards Sarah, and passed right through her chest.

Sarah started to scream and woke with a start. She looked around her bedroom, confused and disoriented, the covers in a pile around her waist.

Early morning light spilled across her room from the double windows on the far wall. Right in its proper place sat her father's bat.

"It was a dream," she whispered, brushing back wild locks of hair from her face.

The clock on her nightstand glowed the time, 6:15 a.m., too early to call Jamie on a Saturday morning. And, although she could hear her mother in the shower, getting ready for another busy day, she knew she couldn't tell her about the dream. This would inevitably end up in a discussion she wasn't ready to talk about.

Something hit the outside of the house just below her window. Sarah hugged herself and rocked to and fro on the bed, reminding herself over and over that it had all been a dream.

She tried her best to believe that that was all it had really been.

Chapter 4

Saturday went from bad to worse in a matter of minutes. Still shaken from her dream, she answered an early morning call from Jamie, who had not chosen to sleep in after all. Her request? She wanted to go back to the cemetery, and Sarah definitely did not want to. In fact, she wanted nothing more than to forget everything about the Specters, the cemetery, those stupid photos, all of it and go about her normal life. But Jamie being Jamie, begged and begged, repeating "Please! Please!" until the only way Sarah could make her stop was to say, "Yes. Fine. Whatever." With the result that Jamie burst into ear-shattering laughter, which was almost worse than her pleas.

Sarah considered telling Jamie about her dream, but second thoughts told her it would be better not to. Pulling on jeans, a sweatshirt, and Nikes, she was ready for Jamie to pick her up.

Perhaps Shane was right in some way about this ghost; maybe it was trying, for whatever reason, to connect to her.

A gust of wind blew rain against the living room windows. Oh great, just what she needed. Not only was it bound to be cold out, but it was pouring too.

Sighing, Sarah slid on her jacket and slipped out into the chilly rain as Jamie pulled up in her mother's Mercedes sedan.

A thin blanket of skin numbing mist cloaked the cemetery as the group gathered, rain drenched, on the dirt road beside the rusted iron fence that lined only half the perimeter.

"This would make a perfect Spielberg movie," Todd said. Cupping his mouth with both hands, he howled like a werewolf.

The fog rose half way up their legs and swirled around their knees. Todd, ever the jokester, waited until Kate walked by and jumped out with a horrible yell.

"You scared the crap out of me, idiot!" Kate shouted, punching him in the gut.

Once again, Sarah was left to her own devices. But this time she wasn't about to stand there looking stupid. As the others mulled about, she ventured off on her own, making her way over graves and trying to avoid tripping over headstones hidden by the thick fog. Time and again, Sarah caught herself looking over her shoulder at the marble monument that seemed to dominate the graveyard. Finally, she paused to kneel down and read aloud the names and dates neatly carved into the weathered stones.

Marilyn Franklin
Beloved Wife and Mother
1792 - 1836.

Andrew Roland Jackson
Died May 5, 1912.

Getting to her feet, Sarah suddenly felt a frigid wind like none she'd ever felt before whipping her wet hair and stinging her eyes. There, at the edge of the thick wood was a woman, her dress sticking like wet plaster to her tall, thin frame. Neither Sarah nor the gaunt woman moved, their eyes locked. Sarah was amazed that, for some strange reason, she felt as though they knew one another. Fear pricked the hairs on the back of her neck, sending a chill up her spine. Deciding that walking off alone was a bad idea, she turned back, ready to join the others only to trip over something and fall face first into the soggy ground.

Rolling over onto her back, Sarah looked up into the steel gray sky above her, realizing that she could no longer hear the voices of her friends, nor could she turn her head. All she could see was gray, the cold wet gray of fog all around her, under her, and above her. When she heard voices - low and muffled - she realized they belonged to two strangers.

She attempted to open her mouth to scream, terrified by the sudden paralysis that held her to the ground. But she could not make a sound. In fact, she couldn't even open her mouth, or move a finger, for that matter.

"Poor thing," someone said in a thick country voice. "Not much more than a child."

"Good God," another man replied. "Who would do such a

thing? Look at her!"

"Better go fetch the Sheriff, Wayne," the first man said.

Sheriff? What was going on? Sarah struggled again to move or to speak and again failed.

"Look at all that blood. Can't even soak into the ground there's so much of it. Do you see it?"

"I see it, Wayne. Now go fetch Sheriff Brewler. He'll be wanting to see this."

The silence that followed was raw and unnerving. An eternity shifted before her, coming and going in waves of colorless mist and through it she could see a shadow bending over her and a calloused hand brushed against her cheek.

"Poor thing," she heard one of the men say. "You're a beauty. Devil of a man who did this to you. I hope he burns in hell for what he's done. God rest your soul." And then the shadow disappeared.

"Sarah! Are you okay?" Suddenly Shane was bending down to help her to her feet.

Sarah couldn't think. She had no idea how to explain what had happened.

"I tripped over something," she said, overwhelmed by relief when she discovered that she could speak.

"We got worried when you just disappeared," Shane said.

All five of them gathered around her. It was clear from their expressions that she had given them quite a fright.

"What happened?" Jamie asked.

"I fell, and then..." but she couldn't continue. She didn't know how to put it into words.

"Did you see something?" Dennis asked.

"Sort of," she told him. "It was very weird. Can we leave, please?"

"Maybe it is time to leave," Kate agreed.

Sarah looked over her shoulder and would have sworn a shadow faded into the darkness of the trees.

Chapter 5

Stretching, Sarah realized that she felt more alive than she had felt in over three days. The night had been silently blissful with no rampaging murderous men, no pale-faced women crying out for help. Not even the crickets or the owls had dared to make a sound. Already, the nightmare was starting to slip back to the nether regions of her mind, and she determined to forget it as well as what happened in the cemetery.

As she waited outside for Jamie to pick her up, she found herself humming a little tune.

"You look radiant this morning," Jamie greeted her as she opened the Mercedes door.

"I feel fantastic!" Sarah said. "I can't even begin to describe how I feel. It's as if I've slept for a week and showered in a fresh mountain spring."

"Gee, what did you dream about last night? Or should I say who?" Jamie asked, winking.

"That's just it, Jamie," Sarah said. "I didn't dream at all! I slept like a baby all night long."

"You know, I never understood why people use that phrase," Jamie said, grinning. "Ever been around a baby? They don't sleep soundly. Newborns are up every couple of hours, then when they get older it's all hush-hush, don't wake the baby."

Jamie pulled off the main road and into the parking lot of the two-story brick building that was Pike High.

"I don't know," Sarah said. "I've seen women walking around with babies who manage to stay out cold no matter how much racket is going on around them. You just weren't so lucky when Jessica was born. And what is it with your mom picking names that begins with J, anyway?"

"Family tradition, I guess. Anyway, enough about babies. You really didn't have dreams or visions or anything last night?"

"No. Why? Does that disappoint you?"

"Well, yeah," Jamie said. "I mean we were going so strong, you know, the photographs and all."

"I don't want to think about it anymore," Sarah said. "You're disturbing my peace." She felt a tightening in her chest. The calmness she had awoken with vanished, replaced by a chill.

"Maybe that's it then," Jamie sighed.

"What's it?"

"I mean, maybe that's it." Jamie shrugged. "Maybe it's over."

As they pushed their way through the massive front doors, Sarah looked over her shoulder, expecting to see the strange woman watching her.

"No," she said. "It's not over."

When lunch came around, Sarah found herself drawn to join the supernatural circle that constituted the Specters, even though they all went on and on about Saturday and how fantastic and incredibly outrageous it was. Only Kate seemed quiet and reserved, and several times Sarah looked around to see that she was watching her. Of the entire group, she thought, Kate was the only one she didn't really understand although, in a strange way, she thought it possible that they were very much alike.

When they were all seated at one of the cafeteria tables, Todd pulled out a folder and opened it. Inside he had a single 5x7 photo from Saturday's adventure. Carefully, he laid it flat on the table for all of them to see.

The photograph showed Sarah with her back to the camera. Although the day had been dark and dreary, Sarah's image was sharp. She was standing with her back to Todd, a ring of black encircling her, broken by a streak of white, long and thin, that seemed to be coming at her from the woods like an arrow.

Everyone at the table sat as silent as they had after seeing the first picture, all looking at Sarah expectantly, clearly waiting for her to say something.

That was when Sarah decided to tell them about the man in her house, as well as the woman who had appeared at the edge of the woods right before she fell, during their last visit to the cemetery. The only thing she didn't tell them about was what had happened when she was in the grass.

"You think he's the darkness and she's the light?" Sarah asked when she had finished.

"It's possible," Shane said.

"But why would they be there at the same time?" Todd asked. Pursing his lips, he blew his shaggy black hair away from his eyes.

"Maybe he actually murdered the woman," Dennis said. "Sarah said he warned her that he'd kill her."

"But why did they seem so focused on Sarah?" Kate asked.

"That's what we have to find out," Shane answered.

Sarah couldn't believe that they were talking about all this as though it were actually true. Oddly enough, she found herself believing they might be right, after all.

Chapter 6

The late afternoon sun fell warm and golden upon them as they sat along the old railroad bridge, their legs dangling above a rocky, weedy stretch of neglected land spread thin like a threadbare blanket.

Sarah listened with half interest as Shane preached about what the Specters stood for.

"This is it, guys. We made a promise when we formed our group. Ghosts are real and their reality is ours for the investigating. We have a clear and strong connection with one, maybe two, ghosts. This is for real," Shane said.

"Where do we begin?" Kate asked.

She was beautiful in an exotic way, small but shapely, with flawless olive skin and rich brown eyes. Beside her, Dennis looked even larger than he was. At five foot eight, he was built like a quarterback. His freckled face gave him boyish charm, and his humor, while sometimes immature, gave him that certain charm. Todd could have been his twin, minus the freckles. But it was Shane who was the real distraction with his movie star good looks, together with blond hair and golden tan. The five of them had been friends most of their lives. Only Sarah was a newcomer.

So many things were new for her. She had moved to Pikesville, started Pike High, and befriended Jamie all in the past year. A new world had seemed to be opening up before her. But now it offered paths that were dark and frightening.

Even though she tried not to remember, she kept thinking of the young woman she had seen in the cemetery, her face so haunted and fair, and the voices she had heard in the mist. She had been pulled into a paranormal wormhole. She felt as though she were caught between two worlds - the past and the present.

What would have happened, she wondered, if Jamie hadn't begged her to go that first day? Would any of this be happening now? Was it fate that she was having nightmares and being caught on film with what appeared to be a ghost reaching out to her?

Sarah sighed as she listened to her friends talk. They wanted to go public. Draw attention to themselves and the truth about life beyond death. Press releases, appearances on the Late Night Show. They wanted it all.

What would happen to her if they did that? Sarah thought

she knew. She'd be ridiculed, criticized, possibly even declared insane and thrown into a mental institute. No, they couldn't go public. They just couldn't. Maybe in ten years, when they were all grown up and established in life, they could whip out these photos and put together one hell of a story. But not now.

Right now she had so many questions. Who was she? When did she live? When did she die? More importantly, *how* did she die? And why was she haunting them now?

Despite her curiosity, Sarah didn't care much for the cold sensation that seemed to grow inside her. Since she had experienced that first grip of something odd, it had refused to let go. Even when she was sitting with friends in the sun, it crept up her spine and settled in every nerve. She wanted to put an end to that. But she also wanted to know this woman's story.

Sarah turned her attention to her friends who were, it seemed, talking about her as if she wasn't even there.

"Hey guys," Sarah said.

Everyone stopped talking. Todd coughed as Kate and Jamie blushed slightly.

"Maybe the ghost needs an answer," She said.

"Like who killed her?" Todd asked.

"Perhaps. Or maybe she just wants to let her family know where she died."

"That's true," Jamie said. "There are hundreds of reports where hauntings suddenly come to an end once the ghost's story is revealed. But where would we even start? We don't even know her name."

"Her name is Emily," Sarah told her. "And we can use the

photograph we have of her to search archives on missing persons and murders. She was found by two men in the cemetery. There has to be some kind of news article about it. We can start there."

As she spoke, she was aware of a warm, tingling excitement.

"What are you talking about?" Shane asked, studying her with suspicious eyes.

"What? I told you about it," she said.

"No," he pressed her. "You told us about the nightmare at home where you were called by the girl's name. Cough it up, girl. What do you know?"

After she had described in detail exactly what she experienced the other day, no one said a word. It gave her goose flesh to even retell the story. She thought she saw gray mist starting to roll across the ground below them, as if coming to claim her, to take her back to that moment when, unable to move, she had been as good as dead.

The silence of the others began to bother her. Were they thinking that she was insane, or that she was making fun of them by coming up with such an outrageous story? She should have kept her mouth shut.

"Well, that settles it then," Shane said, finally. "When Winter Break starts, I say we spend it doing some serious research."

Chapter 7

Winter Break brought with it dry cold air and the promise of the beginning of their project, although the adventure took off slowly.

The library was an old and dusty two-story plaster building. Inside, it held the whispers of long gone librarians and the thousands of students and patrons who had graced its shelves and seats.

The archives were kept in an upstairs storage room where the Specters were given free reign over the old microfiche machines and the yellowing newspapers of Pike County.

But as they pored over the many newspapers and microfiche films they came up empty handed, time after time.

By the end of the first few days, they hadn't found a single article about the cemetery, a murder or even a missing girl named Emily. They were rapidly becoming discouraged.

"I don't understand it," Shane said, stretching his long legs.

"Not a single thing. Nothing, nada, zippo!" Jamie exaggerated her words by throwing her arms up over her head.

"Maybe we need to sleep on it and start again tomorrow," Kate suggested, so exhausted she was glassy eyed.

"I guess so," Shane said, clearly resigned.

It was only when Jamie agreed to spend the night at Sarah's that a bit of the obvious fell into Sarah's lap. Since it would seem that Sarah had the gift to see into this woman's life, what would happen if she actually concentrated and tried to contact the ghost? Of course this meant she would have to slip back into that dark, cold, fatal past and sponge up whatever information she could. It scared the wits out of her, but it seemed the only way.

"Do you think you could really do it?" Dennis asked.

"I think so," Sarah said. "Maybe if I just focus on her, think about her and all the questions we have until I fall asleep, maybe something will happen."

"And you feel comfortable doing this?" Shane asked.

"As long as Jamie is there with me, I'll be fine," she assured him.

Chapter 8

As night came and the house fell quiet, Sarah and Jamie retired to her bedroom and studied the photos they had. Around two o'clock in the morning neither one could keep her eyes open any longer. Tucking the picture of Emily standing by the monument under her pillow, Sarah closed her eyes and slipped into a deep sleep.

The sound of someone moving woke her. Lying absolutely still, she breathed slow and soft, listening. When the sound failed to repeat itself, Sarah sat up, amazed to discover that the pink and blue pajamas she had gone to sleep in were now nothing but a thin cottony nightgown. Suddenly she realized what had happened. She was Emily.

"Oh no. Please no, not tonight," she heard someone say.

Boom! Boom! Boom!

Only then did Sarah realize that the banging was coming from her closed door. Each time it was struck, the door rattled, nearly coming off its hinges.

She looked around, frantic. The window was wide open, a humid summer breeze swayed the dark curtains back and forth. She felt herself float across the room as if she weighed no more than a feather. With a terrified glance behind her, she slipped through the open window and out into the muggy night. Just as her feet touched the cool, wet grass, a man roared, "Emily!"

Turning, she ran as fast as she could, her arms pumping wildly at her sides. Her breath came in painful gasps as she sprinted across the back yard. Several yards from the house, she tripped and fell hard against the dewy grass, making her sneeze. Sarah pushed herself back up onto her feet and looked back at the house.

"Oh my god!" she breathed.

Lit by the milky light of the full moon stood Sarah's own house. She had expected when she was transported into Emily's time and place that everything would be different. And then she realized that there were, indeed, some differences. The house was definitely hers, but the addition that housed her mother's master suite was missing, as well as the flower boxes that they had put in beneath the kitchen windows the first spring they were there.

"Get up and run!" She sounded panic stricken. "He's going to kill you for sure this time. Now get up and run!"

Sarah needed no further coaxing. She had turned her back

to the house once more and resumed her desperate flight towards the woods. At the same time, she heard the kitchen door crash open, slamming so hard against the back of the house that the sound of splintering wood echoed in the still night.

That was when Sarah remembered something. Soon after they had moved in, they had discovered a crack running beneath the kitchen window. Mom had said that she thought it added a touch of the antique, but during their first winter, too much cold air came through and so they had to have it fixed.

Sarah's head spun. Her mind blurred, trying to find coherent thought. She couldn't. Emily's panic was intoxicating. Her terror flooded Sarah's veins like iced honey. The pain in her chest convinced her that there were two hearts racing inside her. One was a young, living, breathing heart while the other was that of a heart which was about to die.

She didn't need to look behind her to know she was being chased, because an evil presence was biting at her heels. And yet she did not sense that it was the same presence that she had struggled with in her house. No, this was something different, something even more terrifying.

As one body with two very different souls, she and Emily ran with every ounce of god-given strength there was to muster, the night whipping at her face, flinging her hair behind her, eyes blinded with tears. Still she ran, only slowing down when she slipped into the velvety black of the woods, twisting and turning along a narrow pathway that somehow she seemed to know.

Her pursuer, on the contrary must have collided with a tree, for something elicited a maddened howl. Still, he did not halt. She could hear him barreling his way behind her.

"You're a dead girl," he called. "I can see you, you little witch."

And he most likely could, she realized, since her nightgown was light and so pale against the darkness that she must have shone like a beacon.

Sarah ran headlong towards a break in the trees. As she came bursting through into a moonlit clearing, she saw that she was in the cemetery, the headstones looming up at her.

And then, with a sudden start, she woke to find herself drenched to the bone with sweat, her pajamas, once more pink and blue, stuck to her like glue, her hair wet at the nape of the neck and along her forehead. Her legs ached, and every time she took in a breath, it hurt. She was relieved when she felt Jamie beside her.

A silvery white haze streamed in through the window in a fat line. Climbing out of bed, her heart still pounding against her ribs, as though she were running still, she walked to the window and stared out into the star dappled night.

This was her room, yet it was Emily's room too. Only a short time ago she had crawled through this very window, running for her life. Sarah shivered. Now she understood why it was she whom Emily had chosen. Just over a year ago when she and her mother had moved into this cozy, little house they had thought they had found a refuge all their own. But now Sarah realized that they had actually found a house ripe with history, a tragic history that involved the death of a lovely young woman. Sarah sighed, staring up at the moonlight streaking its way across the ceiling.

"Good night Emily," she whispered and closed her eyes.

Chapter 9

Sarah and the Specters had become inseparable. They spent nearly every day together, from morning to dusk, and most often until way after sunset. Often they gathered in Sarah's kitchen, where, time and time again, she repeated what they had come to call The Emily Dream in vivid detail.

Had the fear gone away? No, not really. It still lingered at the core of her spine. However, now she was determined to find out who had killed Emily. Her run through the woods had frightened and angered her. Someone evil had been chasing her, as well as Emily. And she knew, deep down, that he had caught Emily and taken her life.

"Let's go back to the library," Shane said. "We'll look one

more time, and then go to the police station and see if they will let us go through some criminal records."

"Like they'd let us do that," Kate scoffed.

"We can tell them we're working on a project," he said. "A murder case. It could work, and we really are working on one."

Back at the library, they invaded the stacks again. Hours went by as they dug deep. Once again they came up with nothing.

They left, ignoring the beauty of the crisp winter day and made their way to the police station, where, to their surprise, they found it not difficult at all to gain access to old files. They were led to a small, dingy room full of mold and shadows, illuminated only by a single 60-watt light bulb hanging inside a wire cage. As they moved around, it swung from side to side, making the shadows dance.

Numerous files surfaced with interesting details about various crimes committed in the town over the years, but nothing that involved the name of Emily.

"What if the crime dates back too far or something?" Jamie asked. "What if it happened before there was a town here, or even a newspaper?"

"Well, there was a sheriff," Sarah said. "He was definitely involved. The two men were going to fetch him."

"Maybe," Shane said. "You can't be one hundred percent certain that everything you see or dream is real and did happen. It's a hard thing to do, keeping reality and your own imagination apart from what's associated with the ghost."

"I know for sure that the sheriff was involved," Sarah said a bit hotly.

"Do you remember his name?" Dennis asked, thumbing through a mildew covered manilla folder.

Sarah thought for a moment, her tongue doing a quick pass over her pink lip glossed lips.

"It began with a B, Bruser - Bower- ugh," she told him. "It's right there on the tip of my tongue."

Images of that fog enshrouded day skipped across her mind, as she returned to the moment when Emily's body was found.

"I have an idea," she said thoughtfully. "It's going to sound weird, but it just might work."

"What can be any weirder than what we're involved in already?" Kate asked.

"I believe I live in Emily's house," Sarah said. "I don't think it was just an overactive imagination that made me have those dreams. When Emily crawled out my window, she ran across the yard and into the woods. I've never been in there. But I seemed to know there was a path, one that amazingly enough, led me right to the cemetery. If we retrace her steps perhaps Emily will come to me and tell me something - some detail that we need to know."

"You really think that you moved into the house of a ghost and that now it can possess you?" Shane demanded.

"Why would you, of all people, think it's not possible?" Sarah countered.

"It's just that all this is getting a bit too Twilight Zone, even for me," he came back at her.

"Did you ever think you'd be living the life of a dead girl, Sarah?" Todd asked, grinning.

"No," Sarah replied. "I thought you were a bunch of freaks trying to corrupt my best friend and that I would be the one to pull her back to sanity."

It was a few seconds before anyone laughed.

"It wouldn't hurt to try it and see if there is a path," Jamie suggested.

"Yeah, I guess it wouldn't," Shane finally admitted.

The brush was extremely dense as they pushed aside the overgrown brambles that seemed to catch whatever they could. Pale ribbons of gold light managed to find a way in, zigzagging here and there through the branches of the pine trees. As they moved deeper into the woods, a silence, thick and foreboding, fell over them.

"I don't see a path," Kate hissed.

"Why are you whispering?" Todd whispered back.

There seemed to be no way a path could exist. The brush dominated the entire earthen floor. Gnarled roots and leaf litter from the enormous oaks mingling with the pine and a horde of small prickly bushes made walking near impossible.

"Over here!" Shane called out.

It was only a memory of a path, nothing more than a narrow strip of earth marred by twisted roots. However, it *was* a path offering entry deeper into the darkness. They hesitated.

"We're going to have to walk single file," Todd said. "I'll take the middle."

Shane took the lead with Dennis bringing up the rear. They walked slowly. No one came right out and admitted it, but they were all afraid. Their fear moved from one to another like a telepathic wave.

Not that they were afraid of Emily's ghost. Instead, they thought about the evil presence of the unknown man who had stormed Sarah's house and knocked her to the floor.

"Hey guys, can you move it a bit quicker up there," Dennis said, looking back over his shoulder for yet another time.

A sudden blast of bitter cold air stopped them dead in their tracks. Jamie grabbed hold of Sarah's shirt and gripped it with all her might, while Kate slammed into Todd's back so hard they both cried out. Spinning around, Shane shushed them. As they waited, barely daring to breathe, Sarah felt a power, raw, biting and unseen and knew that it was hunting them, snaking its way through the trees, hidden by the darkness. She could feel it coming, getting ever more nearer.

"Sarah, do you sense anything?" Shane asked.

"I think I do," she said in a low voice.

"What?" Kate, Todd and Dennis asked as one.

"Honestly? I sense that we better run like the wind and get our butts out of here," Sarah replied, feeling panic rise in her throat.

As if a firecracker had gone off beneath their feet, they tore off down the path, suddenly aware of a rotting stink of mold and decay which seemed to envelope them on every side, making them gasp for breath, making it difficult to run.

Losing his balance, Shane stumbled forward. Sarah shot her hand out and managed to catch the back of his shirt before he went sprawling face first. And then it happened. Like a comedic domino routine, they all fell, Shane first, then Sarah and then the rest, one on top of the other as the cold settled down over them.

"Get off me!" Kate cried out.

"Get your elbow out of my eye!" Dennis said.

Somehow they managed to untangle themselves, desperate to regain their feet and go on running. Tempers rose as they kept stumbling, pulling each other back down over and over again. And then, in the middle of their struggle, the cold air turned arctic and their breath plumed before them in a thick white cloud, the cold biting deep into their bones.

"Where's Sarah?" Shane asked.

Sarah was trapped against a monster of a tree, an inky black shadow spilled from the branches above her.

Chapter 10

Sarah looked to her friends, silently pleading for help. And then that voice, that awful, harsh voice, filled her ears, its breath burned her cheeks.

"Emily," it hissed.

"He thinks she's the dead girl," Todd whispered. Awe had transformed his face into one of boyish bewilderment.

Somehow Sarah swallowed her fear long enough to speak, "What do you want?"

At the sound of her voice, the shadow pulled back slightly before pressing against her once more. Even though she could not see his eyes, she could feel them reaching deep to the center of her soul.

"You little witch. You liar," he hissed again, the pinpricks of his breath stinging her face.

"You are evil!" she said, nearly choking on the words.

All of the sudden the shadow blew apart into a hundred shards of inky black wisps and dissipated so quickly that, for several long moments, Sarah could not believe that the ghostly presence had even been there. But it had. Her cheek, hot and stinging, told her very clearly how real it had been.

But there was no more time to think. In a flash, she was surrounded by the Specters. Jamie hugged her, holding onto Sarah so tight her breath was caught in her throat. Even Shane held onto her, his eyes wide and bright, and for the first time, unsure.

"That was freaking incredible!" Todd shouted.

"Can we discuss this out in the sunlight, please?" Kate asked, already beginning to back up along the path.

Jamie pulled Sarah away from the tree, and they ran headlong down the path and out of the woods. As they burst through the thinning layer of pine and oak, the cemetery came into view.

It was ironic to think that a graveyard could be a place of refuge. But it was.

"Oh geez, look at her cheek!" Kate cried out. "It's burning red as though someone had slapped her."

Sarah raised a shaky hand and caressed the side of her face. The skin, warm and tender, tingled.

"I think reality has just taken a sucker punch," Todd said.

Sarah fell to the ground, not saying a word, while the

others seated themselves around her, their eyes flickered from headstone to headstone, to the ground or the sky. Everywhere except the forbidding trees of the woods. As Todd poked the ground with a stick, Shane sat, chin cupped in his hand, thought fogging his eyes.

"It's not going to stop, is it?" Sarah asked.

How could it? They had no information, no leads, nothing else to go on. It was hopeless. She would live out the rest of her life mixed up in this hellish nightmare.

"Maybe we can find Emily's name on one of these graves," Jamie said.

"It's no use," Sarah said, "she died here but she wasn't buried here. Somehow I'm sure I'd know it if she were."

"The Sheriff," Shane said.

"What about him?" Sarah asked.

"He's our last chance," he told her. "We have to find him."

"You've got to be kidding," Dennis said. "We don't even know how long Emily's been dead. She could be a hundred years dead for all we know. What are the chances of finding a man who could be a hundred years old?"

"It's our only chance," Shane countered. "Do you have a better idea?"

"Yeah, we do nothing about it. Log our photos as evidence of the paranormal, start our fancy collection, go on finding more ghosts and so forth. Why do we even need to know this ghost's life story anyway?"

"Because she is asking me for help," Sarah told him.

"You?" Dennis said. "I thought you didn't believe."

"Well I didn't! But now I have no choice, do I?" Sarah's temper flared.

"Stop it guys," Jamie said, "It wouldn't hurt to do a little more research."

With that said, there was nothing left to do but go back to square one and retrace their steps along history's path. The problem was getting back out of the cemetery so that they could go on with their investigation, because it was painfully obvious that the only way back was through the woods. If they went out the other way to the road, it would take hours to walk back around to Sarah's house. The idea of the darkness, the coldness and the invisible evil stalking them through the trees turned their blood to ice.

"I'm not going back through there," Sarah said adamantly.

Her face had paled to a sickly shade of grayish white and her hands trembled. Her eyes, normally so bright and alive, were ringed with circles so deep that even her long black lashes couldn't hide them.

"Are you going to be all right, Sarah?" Jamie asked, putting her arms around her.

"I am not going through there," she repeated.

"Sweetie, calm down," Jamie said. "It's the only way back."

"Calm down?" Sarah retorted. "Ha! That's funny. I don't see a slap across *your* face. I didn't have to pull you off a tree, where you were pinned by some stinking, vile, *thing*. Calm down? This isn't some bump in the night that goes away at dawn. This thing touched me. It *touched* me!"

"Sarah," Jamie said.

But there was no consoling her. She felt so threatened and

terrified. And worse of all, she didn't know what to do. Tears streamed down her face, leaving black trails of mascara along her cheeks.

"It is the only way back," Shane told her. "I'm sorry but that's the way it is."

"You go back, I'll walk the other way." Sarah spun on him with fire in her eyes.

"Listen to me," he said. "We have to go back. And you have to be strong. This thing can't hurt you. Not if you refuse to give in to the fear of it."

"What do you know?" she asked him.

"I know more than you realize. Why do you think I started this group?" he asked.

"Did your ghost slap you across the face or pin you to a tree or stomp on your back in your own hallway? Did any of your ghosts ever *hurt you*?" she demanded. Clearly none of them knew what she was feeling.

"Well no, but I'm just saying that I know the fear," Shane told her. "That part I have dealt with. Many times."

"Thanks," she finally whispered.

"Come on," Jamie said. "Let's get back before it gets dark. That's something I don't even want to consider."

Once again they entered the woods. Their bodies tight with tension, their breath quick and uneven. The darkness of the forest seemed to cling to them. Fear nipped at their minds. Every sound spooked them. The slightest breeze made them hurry. They trotted single file along the barely visible path, and just when they thought they were in the clear a cold wind, carrying that awful stench, assaulted them again.

"Emily." The word was nothing more than a whisper on the wind, a rattle among the tree limbs, and yet it carried with it a reality that was not their own, one that terrified them.

Forgetting their determination not to be afraid, the six of them bolted down the path. By the time they shot through and rushed down Sarah's backyard, not one of them could catch their breath.

Back in the safety of the house, they collapsed on the closest thing handy, chairs, sofa, even the floor.

"Dear lord what are we going to do about this?" Todd asked. "Man, my legs are like rubber!"

"We hunt for information, that's what we do," Shane replied, resting his head back against the sofa.

Sarah's eyes locked with his and she knew that they were on the verge of something more frightening than she had even imagined.

Chapter 11

They had decided Saturday would be as good a day as any to begin their quest. And, indeed, it proved to provide them with a treasure chest of information. Having met at the library early in the morning, they picked out microfiche, and immersed themselves in the history of their little town.

Pikesville was a small town, even today, set down in the midst of rolling hills, but it had been considerably smaller in the years preceding this one. Either nothing of importance had happened or the newspaper, which had been established in 1930, was not strong on reporting much of anything besides who attended which tea party and the schedule of local events.

As they looked through the microfiche, it became apparent

that it might be difficult to find any information about Emily. Bad things must have happened, but they were not reported. Sarah supposed small towns liked to keep their secrets, keeping their pride intact and the belief that they lived in a perfect little world.

Sarah read and read until the words in front of her blurred. Leaning back in her chair, she let herself slip away to a place inside her where she could be at peace, a place where dead girls didn't talk and mysterious men didn't threaten her. For a few wonderful minutes, she was normal again, just a typical teen-age girl in a typical world. And everything was just the way she liked it to be.

"I found him!" Jamie called out suddenly, jarring Sarah back to reality.

Jamie's screen held the front page of an old newspaper article. The bold black letters stretched across the top edge proclaiming "Sheriff Resigns After Fifteen Years".

They gathered around Jamie as she read the news release out loud.

Sheriff Edmond Brewler, of Pikesville, announced yesterday that he would resign by the end of the month. When asked why he had chosen to give up his badge the sheriff simply replied, "It's time for me to retire." The sheriff has served his community with love, compassion, and dedication for fifteen years. His resignation will constitute a true and great loss to the town. There is no word as of yet on who will be taking his place.

There was a small but very clear picture of a balding man with white hair and kind eyes below the article. A thick white mustache hid his lips, but it was clear that he was smiling.

"Think it's him?" Shane asked, peering closely at the picture.

When Sarah looked more closely, a shock of electricity vibrated up her spine, tickling the back of her neck and raising the hairs on her arm. She didn't need any further reassurance. She sat back.

"That's him," she said. "That's the man that was called to the cemetery the day Emily's body was found. I'm sure of it."

Their excitement flowed right down to their stomachs, and Dennis' stomach let out a lion like roar. Breaking the tension with peels of laughter they agreed to go get some lunch.

The burger shop was packed with families and kids from school. How great it was, Sarah thought, to be out with other people who were talking and laughing as though they didn't have a care in the world. As they ate burgers and fries, they thumbed through an old phone book and found eight numbers listed under the name Brewler. It was Shane who hit the jackpot.

"Edmond Brewler," he said. "Sixth name down the line."

"Do we call him?" Kate asked.

"I say we just drive out there and knock on his door," Shane replied.

"You're too bold, you know that?" Sarah told him, rolling her eyes. "We can't just go knock on his door. What would we say? 'Excuse me, do you know this ghost?' That would go over real well."

"Well calling him will just put him off," Shane argued. "Then if we go knocking on his door, which we all know we're going to end up doing anyway, he can get us for harassment."

"He's right," Dennis agreed around a mouthful of fire-grilled burger.

"Fine, we'll drive out there then," Jamie said. "And we'll take the pictures as proof that we aren't crazy."

Shane grabbed a napkin and jotted down the address.

"Do you think it will really be *the* sheriff?" Kate asked.

"There's only one way to find out," Shane said, putting the phone book in its home beside the pay phone.

Piling into Kate's van, they drove to the address which was more than fifteen miles south of them, barely in the Pike County limits. Sarah sat in the back with the photograph of Emily in her hand. She was nervous, her palms damp and her heart thumping hard in her chest. She felt stupid, afraid, and excited, all jumbled into one emotional bouncing ball. As the others chattered on and on, she had a sense of deja vú, remembering the first time she had joined them. But now, as far as she was concerned, this was more than just an adventure, it was the beginning of their careers as world famous ghost hunters. Or, she feared, something worse.

The night after her ordeal in the woods, she had found herself lying in bed, unable to sleep. Staring up at the shadows that crept across her ceiling, she had struggled very hard to clear her mind of morbid thoughts, but all she could keep thinking was that she was personally connected to all this and that there was a reason why.

Once upon a time she had not believed in ghosts. Once upon a time, she had lived a happy life in a different town with her mother and father and friends and family. Then all that had changed. She had to make new friends, and her mother had done her best to make their new home warm and comfortable.

Once upon a time, Sarah would have scoffed at Fate and all the ridiculous things that Jamie had talked about when they first met. But not now. Now she couldn't even hold onto the conviction that reality was real and ghosts were nonsensical. Now she had to stare Fate right in the eye and figure out what it had in store for her.

What a mysterious power, Fate. It brought lovers together and tore families apart. Her fate was bringing her closer to her friends in a way she had never expected. It had also made it very apparent that there was something special about her. Some kind of fateful circumstance had brought her to a little house out in the boonies and it led her on a path to a forgotten cemetery. And now Fate was demanding that she pay close attention to what it was trying to tell her.

What was the message in this? She didn't know. She wouldn't, not until the very end. If ever an end came about.

"We're here," Kate said, pulling up to a frame house, the front porch of which welcomed them with flower baskets and whitewashed woodwork. All the windows were cracked open, despite the nippy temperatures and the scent of freshly washed laundry filled the air.

"Here we go," Shane said as he opened the side door and climbed out.

A man came out of the door and stood on the first step, watching them curiously. He was not the man from the picture in the library. However, his eyes were kind and very similar to those of the sheriff's, and his hair was a silvery white with just a touch of brown. He had no mustache, true, but his smile was very like that of the man in the picture.

"Mr. Brewler?" Shane asked.

"Yessir," the man replied. "What can I do for you?"

Shane turned and held out a hand to Sarah. In slow motion she handed over the picture.

"Can you tell us anything about this girl?" Shane handed Mr. Brewler the photograph.

Mr. Brewler looked from the picture to the group of kids on his lawn and then back to the photo. His eyes narrowed.

"You kids up to something?" he asked.

"No sir," Shane said, not once losing eye contact. "We're called the Specters, and we're trying to prove ghosts exist and the woman in this photograph decided to help us out. She also led us here to you."

"Is that so?" Mr. Brewler asked.

"It is. You're Sheriff Brewler's grandson, right?" Shane asked.

"You *are* serious," Mr. Brewler said, running a hand through his silvering hair.

"Well, I guess I have good news for you," he said. "It just so happens that I know the story of that young woman. I confess I don't believe in ghost stories and such but I know that this woman had her own demons and I know she died young and by some cruel fate. I've been hearing the same story over and over all my life. And I never needed photos to see her. Grandpops described her so good that she always seemed so real to me. Can I get you kids something to drink?"

Mr. Brewler left them standing on the porch as he disappeared inside and returned with several bottles of Pepsi.

"And now," he said as they all settled down on the front steps, "I'll tell you the story that my grandfather told me."

Chapter 12

"There are stories that slip away little by little so that, by the time the last word is spoken, the story itself has vanished," Mr. Brewler said. "But that lady's story is far from one of those. I couldn't have forgotten it if I had tried. And Grandpops told it over and over and over. Odd thing was, my father never seemed to want to listen to it. I remember when I was very young, my father and Grandpops got into a very heated argument about that girl. Dad became real angry whenever Pops spoke of her. He'd tell him to shut up and once he physically threw Pops out of the house. But anyway, you're not here to listen to my family woes, now, are you?"

Right from the beginning, Mr. Brewler's story was so

fascinating not one of them said a word.

"Her name was Emily Edding," he said. "She had no family. She was a misfit in a time when there was neither room nor tolerance for people who were different. She was alone and wandering and by a cursed twist of fate, she met a man who promised her security. I can only imagine what a gift like that must have seemed to such a lonely young girl. It must have seemed like a miracle from the Lord himself. So of course she took the offer. What foolish child wouldn't?"

"She wasn't a stranger to the town. The folks back then had come to know her and some even liked her. But mostly they only watched her with half interest. She hardly spoke to anyone and kept to herself. Pops called her 'a ghost wandering around in the daylight.'

"Now this man, who told her he'd take care of her, was a mean son-of-a-gun. There wasn't a pleasant bone in his body. He'd scrap with the toughest and lick the blood off his knuckles and walk away laughing. And he was crazy as a loon. Everyone knew that. When word got 'round that he'd manipulated that young girl into living with him, out of wedlock and in sin, no one dared say a word. They figured it'd be better to let them suffer their own when it came to Judgment Day. Farrell Helding wasn't the sort you wanted on your bad side. So they left well enough alone and turned their attention another way."

Sarah's mind slipped through time. She envisioned a slim, young girl wandering about a town where few would meet her eyes. A wave of sadness washed over her. She returned her attention to Mr. Brewler.

"Pops always said he'd wanted to get her away from him. One time he did approach her and offered her an honest job working for him at his house. She said no, of course. There'd be no story today and no ghost in a graveyard if she'd said yes. So life went on.

"Davis and Wayne, now they weren't from around here. They were hired help that summer and I seriously doubt they ever recovered from the shock of what they found that day. But in order to understand the full tragedy of her death, let me tell you what I know of her life.

"Emily suddenly stopped showing up around town," he said, frowning as though what he was remembering was somehow painful. "Farrell's house was somewhere far out in the woods. Pops had gone to his cabin on several occasions when rowdy drunks would go out there, hooting and hollering and threatening to lynch the loon. For a while, people thought her not being around anymore seemed suspicious. Pops got more than concerned and, now and then, he'd go out there to check on her. One day when he went out there he noticed that she was nothing but skin and bones. She was wasting away to nothing. All the while, Farrell was coming into town more and more and drinking up his hard day's pay. He wasn't fighting and causing trouble though. It was more like brooding."

A pile of dry leaves scraped against the ground as a gust of wind passed over.

"One day, about a month or so before she was found dead, Pops saw Emily in town. He said she was looking pretty darn vibrant. He saw her talking to a stranger that day, a tall handsome fellow. It was whispered that she was having a secret romance when Farrell wasn't home. Pops never blamed her any. He felt good that she'd found someone to spark a little life in those dark eyes. He said he wished for her to leave Farrell and find a good, happy home.

"But it wasn't long before Farrell found out about this stranger. And that must have been what changed him from a mean-son-of-a-gun to a murderous one. It wasn't love that pulled his trigger. It could only have been obsession. In his eyes, Emily was like a piece of property and that man was trespassing on his territory. Back then you could shoot at a trespasser with no consequences. But Farrell never shot to warn. No sir. No one knows for sure what he did exactly, but just like Emily, he stopped showing up in town. Pops went back out to his place several times. But the townsfolk rode Pops hard, telling him to mind his own business. The pair of them were trouble and the town didn't need any kind of trouble. So Pops gave in. Something that had haunted him until the day he passed away, God rest his soul."

Mr. Brewler drank down the rest of his Pepsi, wiped his mouth with his hand, then continued his story.

"Weeks went by," he said, running a hand through his hair. "Just enough to wipe away the heaviest of the bad feelings Pops was having about the girl. Then came Davis and Wayne, finding her body in a cemetery directly behind Farrell's property. When Pops saw her, his heart broke into a million pieces. I think guilt drove him to tell this story over and over through the years. Guilt can drive a man insane, you know. He never went insane, but I know he never forgot her.

"I won't go into detail to you kids about what those two field workers found. Let's just suffice it to say it was pure carnage. How anyone could do such a thing and to a pretty young lady is beyond me. Anyway, no one believes Wayne ever did get over it. Pops said that he was never the same, kind of loose in the noggin afterwards."

Mr. Brewler met Sarah's gaze and smiled. She saw

something in his face that bothered her. Something wasn't right.

"Mr. Brewler," she said, "why isn't there any documentation about the murder?" Anger, hot and intense burned deep in her gut, curling her stomach into a tight knot.

"Well," he said, his eyes thoughtful, "as I said, the town didn't want trouble. They didn't want the newspapers of the bigger cities barging in and disrupting their peace. Pops felt so terrible leaving Emily in the claws of Farrell. He should have done something sooner. He admitted that many times over. That's my guess. All my life I've heard this tale and isn't it funny that I never stopped to ask that question?"

"It's sad, that's what it is," Jamie said.

"Indeed it is," he agreed. "But it's more than sixty years in the past kids."

"What happened to Farrell Helding?" Sarah asked.

"No one knows for sure. Pops went out to his cabin, ready to put a bullet between his eyes but he found it empty."

"So that's it?" Shane asked.

"That's it? Good Lord, son! What else do you want?"

"I'm sorry, sir," Shane said. "If you knew why it's so important for us to know about Emily, you'd understand why we want to know as much as we can."

"So make me understand," Mr. Brewler said. "Here's a bunch of kids on my front porch showing me a picture of a girl who died before I was born. Apparently I don't know your story, but I told you mine."

"Did they have any children?" Sarah asked.

"No," he told her. "And thank God for small miracles."

When they couldn't think of anything else to say, Mr. Brewler saved them from the awkwardness that settled over them.

"So are you going to tell me what brings you out here? Other than that photo I mean." And then looking from the photo to Sarah and back again, he said, "She's reaching for you, isn't she?"

"It seems so, plus *he* has invaded my house and slapped me across the face," Sarah replied.

"Dead people don't abuse young ladies," Mr. Brewler said. He grazed over them with a suspicious eye before adding, "Some games are neither funny nor fun, let it go, kids."

"We aren't kidding around sir," Shane said. "We all saw it. Look at the photo, isn't that Emily?"

"I can't say for sure who that is," Mr. Brewler said. Standing up, brow creased, he turned his back on them and slammed the front door.

"That was a sudden switch in mood," Kate said.

"At least we know who killed her," Dennis said.

"Yeah, but is it enough?" Todd asked.

"It's going to have to be, for now," Shane said. "Come on, I think we overstayed our welcome."

As her friends walked back to the van, Sarah remained on the porch a few moments longer. She wanted to knock on the door and demand more.

"Sarah," Jamie called out.

Reluctantly, Sarah walked away from the house and climbed into the van.

Sarah turned her face to the horizon where the sun seemed to be sitting on the edge of the world. Was that what it was like to be a ghost, awesome and yet untouchable?

Well apparently not, at least two ghosts could be touched. And they could touch her. When she thought of Emily as she had been, she saw a young woman shining with love. She also saw a very handsome man, several years older than Emily, with eyes as clear as the summer sky and a smile just as warm.

"We forgot to ask about the other guy," she said suddenly.

"What other guy?" Kate asked, pulling onto the highway.

"The man Sheriff Brewler saw talking to Emily in town. The one everybody thought she was having an affair with," Sarah said, frowning at the cars that were speeding by.

No one seemed interested in the stranger. Sarah, however, knew it was a mistake to overlook him. If her hunch was right, there would come a time when they would *have* to take him into consideration.

Chapter 13

The next Monday, school began again, but classes were nothing more than a blur now as far as Sarah was concerned. Nothing was as important to her now as Emily. She stole into her dreams. She stood in every corner. She was every shadow. Watching and waiting, she invaded Sarah's life. Meanwhile winter rolled into spring. And before she knew it, it was summer.

The Specters greeted their freedom of summer vacation with heavy spirits.

"We're forgetting who we are," Shane muttered. "We aren't detectives. We're kids who hunt ghosts, sure, but not murder investigators. We've been focusing too much on Emily and what have we gathered? Nothing. We've forgotten our mission as the Specters."

"We've been doing serious work," Sarah protested. "That's part of the Specter's mission, isn't it? Emily is a ghost remember? We're working on her, for her."

"But we aren't gathering more evidence on other ghosts," Shane reminded her. "We've narrowed our sights and our skills down to one situation. That is not what we're about."

"What are you getting at?" Sarah asked him suspiciously, dreading the answer she knew she didn't want to hear.

"We need to go back to ghost hunting," he said. "We need to give Emily a break."

Everyone but Sarah nodded in agreement.

"Wait, wait," Sarah said, knowing she had to fight for Emily, to keep them focused. "Think about it. We don't have just one ghost here. We have two. Two very unique ghosts haunting in two very different ways."

"But what else is there to do?" Jamie asked.

"How about we go back to the woods and take some footage in there," Sarah said.

After their last experience in the woods, these were the last words Sarah thought she'd ever say. Yet, she needed to convince them.

"I'm serious," she told them. "If we can catch two ghosts on film wouldn't that go towards our mission?"

"Our mission? As in We, including you?" Shane grinned a wicked grin. "I thought you didn't believe in this ghost crap."

When they all broke out into laughter, she joined them. It felt good to laugh. It reminded them that they were still alive and still able to have fun.

"So? Do we go or not?" Sarah asked when their laughter had settled to a few lasting giggles.

"It wouldn't hurt." Shane said. "Everyone in favor say 'aye."

The ayes were unanimous.

They spent the rest of the day with their Nikons singing to the sunset. It felt awesome to work again. All the digging about in the past and the speculation of murder had been a downer. As they took over Sarah's yard, they captured everything. Windows, trees, shrubs, every flower daring to poke its head up out of the neatly mown grass became victim to the camera's scrutiny.

Then it was time to photograph in the woods. Setting their cameras to low light setting, they moved cautiously forward, no longer certain of what would or could happen. Life had opened up a new and bizarre path, and instead of straying from it, they plunged straight down it. The blinding white flashes sent birds scattering out from their shelter. While on and on they went. Moving around trees, down the narrow path, not quite to the cemetery and then back again. Once all of their film was spent, they hopped into their cars to join up again at Jamie's house. Once there, they crowded into her dark room and set about developing the film. This was the best part, for Sarah, to create light and image out of nothing.

Soon the fine ropes zigzagging along the ceiling were filled with dangling photos, hanging from wooden clothespins. They looked from one to the next hoping to find some trace of Farrell Helding. As fate would have it, they were not to be disappointed.

Most of the films showed nothing more than a black

speck here or there. Orbs floated across many of the pictures. Nothing significant. However, in one set, a specific dark orb seemed to be floating. When the photos were placed one atop the other and flipped, it swam up from the left bottom corner and across to the upper right corner of the last photo.

They had marked their own films with their initials on the back so they could log who had caught what. This had been caught by Todd's camera.

"What do you think?" he asked.

"Well, it's an orb," Shane admitted. "And it was moving, but that could be just energy. Critics would say that it could be dust, a bug, reflected light, and so on. We all know the facts."

"Take a look at what Sarah caught," Dennis said grimly.

They couldn't be one hundred percent certain, but any one of them would throw their money on the table that what they saw was real. The man, enormous, dark and very formidable, stood by the same tree to which Sarah had been pinned that dreadful afternoon. Faceless and massive, he just stood there, his body almost as thick as the tree, a shadow among the shadows.

The Specters passed the photo around. Sarah refused to touch it, letting Dennis claim it back. Their excitement danced around her in chaotic chatter. Deep inside she felt cold and shaky, unable to share their amazement.

"Hey, what's that?" Kate asked, pointing to a light spot to the right of him.

"It looks like a piece of a dress or something," Jamie said.

"It's Emily," Sarah said, her breath catching in her throat. She had caught both of them in one shot.

"How can it be Emily?" Dennis asked, frowning.

"Look at it," Sarah said. "It's definitely part of a dress and its drifting by Farrell. It's as if Emily was passing right by him, quickly too."

She ran a finger along the thin streak of light.

"But how can that be?" Dennis repeated.

"Emily's spirit is caught between the house and the cemetery," Todd explained impatiently. "If this man is Farrell Helding then his spirit is trapped in the woods. That's simple enough."

"But how could that happen if he killed Emily," Dennis persisted. "How can their spirits be locked in the same place?"

"Who says they had to die at the same time or in the same spot to haunt the same general area?" Sarah asked.

"That's the rule of haunting," Dennis said. Something was clearly bothering him. He was, Sarah noted, wearing the expression he always wore when he couldn't figure something out.

"Really?" Sarah said, unable to resist. "I didn't think there were rules to haunting."

"The common conception," Shane explained in his usual know-it all way, "is that a place that is haunted by several ghosts all share the same tragic death. Fires, earthquakes, murders, et cetera."

"But *is* it possible that they died separately and Farrell came back to where he killed Emily?" Sarah asked. "That makes sense to me."

"I guess it's possible," Shane said. "But wouldn't that put him in the cemetery?"

No matter how long they debated it, they were at a loss as to how to explain Farrell's existence. When Sarah had encountered him the first two times, she had figured she was living out Emily's experience. It was only on a whim that she offered to take pictures in the woods. She hadn't really thought they'd actually catch him. And now that they had...

"I hate to say this guys," she said, "but maybe we have to learn both sides of the story to put an end to all of this."

Five sets of eyes glared at her.

"Both sides?" Todd exclaimed, throwing his hands up in the air in exasperation. "We know both sides. Emily fell in love with a stranger; enraged with jealousy Farrell killed her. End of story."

"That's only what we were told," Sarah said. "Nobody knows for sure, right? Nobody but Emily and Farrell."

Hotly, Todd said, "but there's this problem of the fact that they are both dead!"

"Give me a moment, would you, Todd?" Sarah said. "What if, after he killed Emily, he was eaten alive by guilt for the rest of his life so that when he died his spirit came back to the woods, as if the woods have become his own private hell. He's chained to the spot where he committed his worst sin. That makes sense, doesn't it?"

She was, she realized, feeling all funky and wild inside. She had to make them see. She just had to make them understand that they had to keep going on this.

"Oddly enough, it does make sense," Shane said.

"But again," Dennis demanded, "wouldn't that put him in the cemetery? What are we doing with all of this? We have two ghosts. So what about how they died!"

"Isn't it the mission of a ghost hunter to learn the reasons *why* ghosts haunt?" Sarah fired back. "Because if it is, then we have to learn their stories in order to answer that question."

"Guys, she's right," Shane said, looking at Sarah with respect and she knew that he could relate to what she was feeling.

"Thank you, Shane," Sarah said. "At least someone can understand."

"We all understand, Sarah. We just don't want to waste all our time on this," Kate said.

"Why not?" Sarah said. "Think of all the things we can learn. Think of the experience it will give us. Besides, what will you accomplish if you only go half way? Nothing!"

She was winning. She knew it and she loved the feeling. Excitement tingled up her spine and filled her with warmth and energy.

"All right for Pete's sake!" Dennis flung himself down in a chair. "We get your point!"

Although she won this battle, something inside of her churned her stomach. A bitter taste coated her tongue, her mouth suddenly very dry. She should be jumping with joy, instead she felt like what Pandora must have felt, when she realized the consequences to opening the mythical box.

Chapter 14

That night Sarah watched TV with her mom for a while before deciding to go to bed. Changing into her pajamas, she lay there, her mind churning as she thought of her father and how much she missed him. She thought of how lonely she had been until she had become part of the Specters. It felt good to have so many close friends to confide in, laugh with and enjoy life together.

Then she thought of Emily. Had she really had no one? What must it have been like living that way? It must have been a blessing for her to find Farrell. At least, with him, she experienced some kind of companionship. That must have been a good thing.

Yet something had gone terribly wrong. Instead of happiness, she found death. And what about that vision, when leaving Mr. Brewler's? She had seen Emily bright with life and with love. Once again, something must have gone horribly wrong.

"What happened, Emily?" Sarah whispered to the night.

With her eyes glued to the ceiling, she recapped Mr. Brewler's story. Little was said about that stranger, a sentence, maybe two, about how the Sheriff saw them together briefly in the street. Every finger pointed at Farrell Helding. And why not? He had apparently been a sour, mean man with a good number of enemies in every direction. Another man, someone who had a pleasing disposition wouldn't have aroused suspicions. But had anyone thought of suspecting that stranger when they had found Emily's body? Or had it been easier to place the blame on Farrell? Especially since he had just seemed to disappear.

That was what bothered Sarah. Even though she knew for certain that Farrell had been the man who had attacked her, she wasn't sure about whether he had killed Emily. Granted that Farrell was an angry man. But simply because of that, how could anyone say that the stranger had nothing to do with it after all? Where had he been when Emily was found? Had he been seen again afterwards? Had he come forward and told the Sheriff anything about himself, and his part in Emily's life? Had there even been a stranger at all?

And what was it that Farrell had kept screaming at Sarah? Liar. Yes, that was it. He had kept calling her a liar and a witch, which must have meant that whatever she had done, it offended him terribly. Still, if Farrell had been drunk, he could have imagined anything. Yet, he had sheltered her. Perhaps he had fallen in love with Emily and then she had betrayed him.

Sarah sighed. Closing her eyes she drifted off for a moment then opened them again. A long thin shadow moved across her ceiling as a cloud sailed across the sky, obscuring the moon.

"I need more, Emily. I need to know what you know," she said as her eyes began to close again.

Suddenly, she was standing in a meadow. Violets and dandelions bobbed their heads in the breeze. The air was sweet and thick with the warmth of the sun.

Sarah danced among the flowers, light hearted and truly happy. For the moment, she was Emily. Maybe tonight she'd learn all the answers to those nagging questions. Perhaps she'd learn how to free Emily from her torment and let her find peace.

Just as the sun began to kiss the horizon she saw a man coming toward her through the grass with quick purposeful strides. He had eyes like the summer sky and a smile that melted her heart. When he reached her he grabbed her hands and they spun around together until they were both out of breath. They tumbled to the ground laughing and holding onto each other.

So this was Emily's stranger. When he lowered his face and kissed her gently, Sarah's heart fluttered. Her skin tingled from head to toe. Oh, how wonderful Emily had felt! Love poured through her like a river. She knew what it was to feel beautiful in someone else's eyes. The feeling intoxicated Sarah.

As evening fell, thick and cloudy, the meadow became empty and cold. She was now alone and terrified. She tried to call out, but her voice fell silent within the void.

The intensity of her feelings suffocated her. Sarah gasped

for breath, gripping the sheets in a vice like hold. She fought against the dream, trying to break free. She did not like this, not at all. Sarah scrambled to awake and felt, instead, that she was sliding back down into the dream, down into the darker side of Emily's life.

Farrell Helding stood on the edge of the void now, his massive bulk unmistakable, even in the gloom. His shoulders spread wide and thick, showing an impressive expanse of muscled chest. His large, thick hands reached out for her.

She went to him, torn between the harshness of her loneliness and the temptations that he offered. Strength showed itself in his brow and set of his jaw, and in his strange, gray eyes.

Crossing the sea of sadness, she allowed herself to become engulfed in his embrace. When he held her, he was surprisingly gentle, burying his face in her hair. She could smell a subtle aroma much like soap and musk.

"Please, Emily," he said in a gravelly voice. "I love you."

She shivered and the entire void quaked as if ready to rip open.

This man loved Emily. He had offered her not only his home but his heart as well and he was, Sarah knew, more vulnerable than he appeared.

The truth shocked her and she dove deeper into sleep, willing the dream to continue. It was a different feeling than the one in the field with the shining stranger. Yet this man's love was just as intoxicating, so ripe, full and overflowing. As if - as if he had never loved before and Emily had been the one and only.

She looked up into his face and had just begun to speak

when a sudden bolt of lightning ripped apart the dream. The stranger, tall and lean and unbelievably handsome stood nearby. Upon his face was a mask of utter hatred, stark and frighteningly vivid.

Sarah awoke to the sound of her own scream.

Chapter 15

Something wasn't right. The nightmare had so shocked Sarah that all she could do was pace around the house. Going to the kitchen, she poured herself a cup of cold milk. While sitting at the table, she memorized every detail of the photograph of Farrell's essence and that drifting piece of dress. Holding it between her fingers, she stroked the little bit of Emily that she had captured. But she did not touch the orb that was Farrell. Oh no, she'd had enough of him. Maybe, just maybe, Emily would give her something more. Perhaps, through her fingers, she'd pick up something, like a vision, telling her more. That's all that mattered to her anymore. Emily.

She looked over at the clock above the oven and discovered

that it was only three in the morning. She thought about her mother, peacefully sleeping in the other bedroom, and a smile crept across her face. Then, just as quickly as it had come, the smile vanished.

What happened to Emily's family? Sarah wondered. Why was she a misfit? She contemplated calling Jamie, so that they could talk about it, but resisted the urge. Jamie couldn't help her find the answers. Then again, she would be someone just to talk to. Sarah was just reaching for the phone when the front door opened and slammed shut.

"Mom?" Sarah said.

Silence answered her. After several moments of hearing only her own breathing, Sarah figured she was just tired and her mind was playing tricks on her. Making her way back to her room, she heard the sound of someone walking through the living room.

"Oh no," she whispered, recognizing the footsteps.

"Emily!" he called.

A shadow moved along the living room wall, just visible from the angle she was standing at.

"Emily, I want to talk to you," Farrell said.

His voice bounced off every wall. She could not escape it.

"Emily, please," Farrell said, his voice softer.

What drove the last spike of panic into her was the fact that his tone was exactly as it had been in her dream, soft, reassuring, pleading. It was the voice of the love that she now knew he had felt only for Emily.

Sarah tiptoed across the kitchen and crept up behind the massive black shape taking up the entire hallway. Everything about him was so unreal. The way he moved, liquid and out of sync, as if parts of him weren't connected the way they should be. He stopped suddenly halfway down the hallway. Mesmerized, she watched as he bent over and picked up something off of the floor. She could feel the heat of rage radiate through him.

"He was in my house!" he roared. "Emily, you liar! You witch!"

Suddenly he had become the truly mean man of Mr. Brewler's story. His temper had flared in the blink of an eye. Clearly, it was a hot temper, and a dangerous one. But was it a murderous rage?

It took a moment for Sarah to realize that the very spot he was standing on was the same spot he had pinned her to during their first encounter with each other. And he was repeating those awful words, saying that he didn't like games.

He called for Emily again but she neither answered nor showed herself. The first night, Sarah had seen a manifestation of Emily come down the hallway, crying and asking for help. Shouldn't she be coming down the hall by now?

With a bear-like bellow, Farrell spun around and bolted out the back door, the force of him throwing Sarah back against the wall. There was no time to think. She only knew that she couldn't let him go. Grabbing the flashlight off the counter top, she ran out the door and into the night. The grass, wet and cool, slapped her bare feet and licked her ankles. Farrell was nowhere in sight.

"The woods," Sarah said out loud. "Of course."

She ran, a thin yellow beam of light leading the way. Pushing past the bushes and the long spindly arms of the pine trees, she headed straight for the narrow path. Though terror weakened her legs, knees wobbling, threatening to collapse, she couldn't stop. She ran on until, after several yards, she came to a sudden halt. Farrell stood near the tree of unbelievable size. The two shapes melted into the darkness.

As she watched, silent and motionless, Farrell grunted and cursed. His body twisted in an apparent frenzy, swinging his arms left and right, kicking out as though he were in a struggle to the death. And then he fell to the ground, his head slumped forward, his arms limp by his sides.

Sarah trained the light on him. She could see him clearly now, not as a ghostly apparition, but as a man. His face was handsome in a rugged way, despite the deep gash that opened wide from his temple to below his ear. Blood poured down the side of his face, his thick, curly dark hair sticking to the sides of his face and neck. He looked at her with large, emotional eyes, tears mixing with the blood. Sarah had never seen so much blood.

"Emily," he whispered, his voice as shattered as his broken face. "I loved you."

Then he faded into nothingness.

Sarah couldn't get her legs to move. Her hands shook so bad that the batteries in the flashlight rattled.

A slow and painful realization took hold of her, rising to a peak and crashing down, bringing with it a terrifying truth.

"Oh my God," Sarah said. "You couldn't have killed her. You died first. That's why you are trapped between the house and the woods. He killed you first."

Finally, forcing her legs to move, she ran back to the house. There was nothing that could stop her from calling Jamie now.

Inside, she bolted both doors and latched all the windows. She sat on the sofa, phone cradled in her arms. With her knees drawn up to her chin, she rocked back and forth.

Mr. Brewler's story must have been a lie, because Farrell hadn't killed Emily. Someone else had killed them both.

Chapter 16

Sarah managed to wait until the sun crested the sky before calling the rest of the gang. She said little, just that they all needed to get their butts over to her house immediately. Once they were all there and seated around her living room, she began.

"You're crazy," Dennis said. The look on his face said he wasn't kidding.

Sarah stared him down. She was not going to waver. Not when she knew for a fact that she was right. She knew it, and she *was* going to make them understand, no matter what it took

"You really believe this?" Jamie asked.

Sarah spun on her heel to face her.

"You think I'm crazy too? Why, because none of you are having weird dreams or dead men storming through your house? So that makes me crazy? I didn't ask for any of this! You begged me to come with you to the cemetery. Remember?" She pointed a shaking finger at Jamie. Her anger so violet it frightened her. She took a deep breath.

"I think you could be right," Shane said.

"We have to go back and ask Mr. Brewler about the stranger," Sarah said.

"I never said you were crazy," Jamie said. "You're caught in the middle of something really strange."

"You're in a tough situation, Sarah," Shane agreed. "You have a gift. Some people find it early as little kids and their parents pass it off as an over active imagination. For some of us, it comes later, unexpectedly. You have to believe in yourself, even when others don't," he added, throwing Dennis a cold look.

"Maybe she's a medium," Kate said. "A channeler."

"I don't know what I am," Sarah said. "But I know that this changes things drastically and it's even more important than ever that we solve it."

"Oh, here we go again," Dennis said, exhaling loudly.

"You don't have to be a part of this," Jamie said.

"Tell me, Dennis, why do you think I'm crazy?" Sarah insisted. "Why can't I be right about this? You believe in ghosts, don't you?"

"Yes, of course I believe in ghosts," Dennis said. "But come on, you're going to tell me that you can actually see their lives unfolding, in your hallway or in the woods, in the middle of the night? I believe you can see them. But I can't believe that you can unravel their lives and solve murders."

"Why can't she?" Shane demanded. "How often are psychic mediums employed now to help investigators solve cases? It's all around us. Society is just now opening up its mind and eyes to the truth. Sarah may be one of those special people."

"I don't know," Dennis said. "It's kind of way out there."

"Why? Because it's one of us this time and not someone on the news?" Jamie asked.

"I say we should pay another visit to Mr. Brewler," Shane said. "Just to see what he can add to his story. It wouldn't hurt and it would give us something to do."

As always he was the voice of reason, Sarah thought. When Shane made a decision, the rest went along.

When they pulled up into the driveway the porch was empty and the front lawn was bare, except for a yellow and green riding lawn mower.

"Let's go up and knock," Shane said, walking up the path and taking the stairs two at a time.

Classical music flowed through the open windows. Shane knocked four solid thuds onto the wooden panel of the door. After a couple of seconds, the volume was turned down and they could hear someone padding across the floor. The thin white curtain hanging over the window swung to the side and Mr. Brewler greeted them.

"Well, isn't this a surprise," he said, holding the door open as they made their way in one at a time. "You kids aren't giving up are you? Let me go fetch something for you to snack on."

He disappeared into the kitchen and came back with a tray of crackers and cheese and more bottles of Pepsi.

"We won't keep you long," Sarah said. "We just have a couple of questions about the stranger."

Mr. Brewler stopped in mid step. He cocked his head, eyeing Sarah curiously. His stare was so intense that it made her uncomfortable.

"The stranger, eh?" he asked.

"Yes. The one your grandfather saw talking to Emily in town one day. What happened to him? Was he ever seen again after the murder? Do you know his name? Was he ever questioned?"

"Whoa, missy. One step at a time," Mr. Brewler said. "In case you haven't noticed, I'm no spring chicken and my mind doesn't run as fast as yours. Now, let me see. No, Pops never got his name. And no, he was never questioned, or else there would be a name. As to what came of him, well no one paid any mind. Why would they?"

"Because he killed Emily and Farrell," Sarah said in a matter of fact voice.

"Is that so?" Those sharp eyes narrowed, as though they were boring a hole right through her head.

Sarah didn't flinch. Instead, she stared back, eye to eye.

"You know what?" he said. "I'm going to tell you something. I don't know why I am going to, but there is something about you. Pops told me something once, when he was dying. Why he told me, I haven't a clue. Dad was there, too, you see. But Pops waited until Dad left the room before he grabbed me by the arm and bent me low so he could whisper his last words into my ear. And what he said was, 'I didn't do right.' When I asked him what he was talking about, he just said it again."

Mr. Brewler frowned, wrinkles creasing his brow. With a quick glance around the room, he made sure everyone was paying attention.

"He died minutes later," Mr. Brewler continued, "his hand in mine. I always figured he was just clearing his conscience because he hadn't done more to catch Farrell. You know, maybe it was his way of coming to terms with his own guilt. Now here you are, again, telling me that someone else killed Emily and Farrell. You know things you shouldn't know, and you have pictures of a girl you shouldn't have. It all gets me to thinking. You know what?"

"What?" Sarah asked.

"When you solve this, let me know what really happened," as he said this, he leaned forward, speaking to Sarah as though she was the only other person in the room. A strange electrifying energy seemed to pass between them.

"Now, if you'll excuse me, I have more mowing to do," Mr. Brewler said, getting up. "Grass grows faster than I can cut it, but what do you do?"

"Thank you," Sarah said. "Thank you very much for all your help." She laid her hand gently on his arm as they walked out the door.

"Just remember me when you glue all the pieces together," he told her, smiling a warm and rather endearing smile. It was the kind of smile that she imagined winning many a lady's heart.

"Things we shouldn't know," Kate said once they were all in the van. "What an odd thing to say."

"We really shouldn't know any of this," Jamie said. "The whole thing should have died with Emily a long time ago."

"You think the sheriff really wondered about the other guy?" Todd asked.

"Why would Mr. Brewler lie?" Shane asked. "He seems honest enough. Besides, I don't think he would have told us if it wasn't true."

"Not *us*," Dennis said, "We didn't even exist, only Sarah."

"Yeah, that was weird," Kate said.

Dennis cleared his throat, speaking up again but making sure to avoid Sarah's eyes.

"If his own grandfather doubted the circumstances, then maybe Sarah's on the right track," he said.

"Is that an apology?" Sarah asked him, grinning.

"Crazy people tend to have bizarre talents," Dennis said with a smile.

Later that afternoon, Jamie and Sarah shared some old-fashioned, best friend time in her room, talking about everything under the sun as they riffled through the photographs.

"We've been through these a hundred times," Jamie complained, stretching to release a cramp in her lower back.

"I know, but look again. There might be something here that we missed. Maybe..." She broke off as Jamie cried out and let out a gasp as she saw, etched in the window, Emily. One hand pressed firmly against the smooth glass. In that hand was a book. Small and leather bound it had neat black writing scrawled across the cover.

"What is she holding?" Sarah whispered.

Jamie shook her head, her eyes wide as saucers.

"What is it, Emily?" Sarah asked, getting up off the bed.

"Don't talk to her!" Jamie squealed.

"She's not going to hurt us," Sarah said.

"This is too freaky. Way too freaky!" Jamie chanted.

Sarah moved closer, one step at a time until she was almost to the window. But as soon as she reached the window, Emily's face disappeared. The only thing left was the quickly fading impression of the book still pressed against the glass.

"I think it was a diary," Sarah said, sitting back down on the bed.

Sarah stared at the window, a warm flush coloring her cheeks. Emily had been there, right in front of them both. And she hadn't been sleeping. She wiped her damp hands on the comforter.

"Did she look familiar to you?" Jamie asked.

"What? No, I don't think so."

"Yes, she definitely looked like someone we know," Jamie said.

"Maybe that's the link," Sarah said, creating a downpour of photos as they hit the floor. "Her diary is somewhere in the house. Maybe even in this room. Get up, help me look."

They tore the room apart, looking in every corner, every crevice. They pulled out the furniture and removed everything from the closet, and came up empty handed.

Finally, lifting up the corner of the dust ruffle, Jamie crawled under the bed.

"What's this?" she asked, her voice muffled.

"What?" Sarah came over and knelt down beside her.

No wonder they hadn't seen it before. Perfectly camouflaged in the natural wood of the floor was a tiny, flat trapdoor, no bigger than a lunch box, the far left corner of which was slightly indented. They pushed the bed aside so they could have full access.

"Give me a quarter or something," Sarah said, picking at the corner.

Jamie fetched a quarter out of the change bowl on the dresser. Carefully placing the quarter in the little notch, Sarah pushed and with a groaning pop the panel gave way to reveal a shallow hole. Inside that hole was hidden a thin leather bound book with neat handwriting in black ink permanently etched into it.

Emily Edding.

"I don't believe it," Sarah said. "It's her diary. She wanted us to find it and we did!"

Chapter 17

Sarah wasted no time in calling the Specters to meet at her house, particularly since her mother was out of town at a conference.

"Bring all your equipment," she told Shane.

Sarah felt it appropriate to set up in her room. After all, it was Emily's room, the room where they'd found the diary. She was impressed by the sophistication of Shane's video equipment. His ingenuity when it came to videography was mind-boggling, particularly when it came to operating his Cannon Mini DVD camera that he carefully set atop the tripod before hooking up the bright white lights.

Sarah perched on the edge of her bed with the diary in

her lap while Todd, Dennis and Jamie manned the three still cameras evenly spaced around the room. As for Kate, she sat cross-legged in the corner, a pad of sketch paper and charcoal pencil in hand.

Shane left no room for mistakes, arranging things so that each camera would catch the scene from every possible angle so that not one inch of Sarah went unfilmed. There was even a voice recorder stashed at the foot of the bed so that he could capture every sound.

They were about to dive into the past and reopen the life of a young woman who had been brutally murdered by someone who may have loved her very deeply. And to do that, they had to know who the stranger had been. They had to know everything because, otherwise, two lost souls would never be put to rest.

"Ready?" Shane asked, one eye looking up over the camera.

"Not really," Sarah answered.

She was, she found, terrified by what she might have unleashed.

The past is the past and it's gone, she thought, looking down at the leather-backed journal. However, this time it wasn't, Emily had come back for her help.

In the last moments of the summer sun, Sarah tried to call on Emily. She pulled forward everything that had happened so far, within her mind. And as she did, she realized how much she had changed herself. In less than a year her entire life metamorphosed from that of an average teen into something much more complicated.

The truth was that she had grown emotionally as a result of all of this. And that growth allowed her to feel in ways she could not have done in ordinary circumstances.

As she sat there, she called for Emily, channeling the young woman with her heart and mind. She would speak the words Emily wrote, she would reveal life as told by the one who lived it. Already, she was beginning to feel a cool, dry energy envelope her. Emily was in the room. Sarah could feel the ghost's emotional turmoil as it collided with her own.

Breathing deeply, she convinced herself she could do this. She had to; she needed to learn the truth.

"Are you ready, Emily?" Sarah whispered.

"What?" Shane asked, looking up from making the final camera adjustments.

"Just asking if you were ready," Sarah told him.

"I'm waiting for you," he said.

There seemed no reason to delay. She would never be any more ready and although Emily had an eternity to wait, it seemed cruel to make her do so. When Shane gave her a thumbs up, she opened the book, and caressed the yellowed pages gingerly.

The first page was blank. Careful not to rip the aged paper, she turned the page and saw Emily's neat writing scrawled across the pages from top to bottom. Sometimes it squeezed in as if it had been written with frantic haste.

"There aren't any dates," she said. "It's just page after page of writing."

"That's okay," Shane said. "Just start reading from the beginning."

Sarah flipped back to the second page. Clearing her throat, she gave one last look around the room, at her friends. And began reading.

It was a long train ride from the convent to Pike County, and I already miss Sister Maria. The Women's House is just as Sister Maria described it. Madam Laura is a very kind woman and she welcomed me in immediately. I've been given a good room with a bed and an armoire.

This is a small town, very quaint and quiet. Even the inn across the street seems to mind its manners. I wish I did not have to leave the convent. But I am sixteen now, too old to be secluded there. Since I cannot become a nun, I have no other option. Sister Maria blessed me the other morning, right before I left. We prayed, asking the Lord to grant me safe travel and happiness. Now that He has granted me safe travel, I must wait to see what life in this little town will yield. I know no one here who can guide me.

Sarah turned the page. Taking in a deep breath she tried to ignore the chill that crept along her spine. But it did no good. She felt as though she were caught in some kind of emotional vise. Finding her voice, she continued.

Saturday at dinner, Madam Laura has announced that she will be leaving. She has sold the house to an old teacher by the name of Ms. Terrance. Madam Laura will not even be here for Christmas. There is

dire need for her back home in Mississippi.
I will miss her dearly. But I fear what
Ms. Terrance will bring down upon this
house.

I have met her once, about a week ago.
She was a harsh woman who wore a dark,
drab dress. Already five girls have promised
to leave. Annie and Marylou have found
work, both at the Major's home. They will
tend to the children and the house. Pay is
low but they will receive room and board
and are promised free time to read, sew and
even learn mathematics, Marylou's passion.
Nina, however, has decided to work in a
brothel eleven miles south, although she
is only seventeen. Despite Madam Laura's
protests, she has already left.

Sarah put the book down. Frowning, she looked up at Shane.

"What is it?" he asked.

"There are major time gaps in here," Sarah said, studying the next page. "She seems to be working for Ms. Terrance on this page."

"Don't worry about it," Shame said. "Just keep reading."

After being nothing more than an unpaid
house servant, I can take no more of Ms.
Terrance's cruelty. Since she took over
the house, I have been forced to give up
my room, and all of my belongings except

for a few unfashionable dresses and hose and one pair of shoes. I scrub floors, walls, and her and her niece's clothing all day long. I have no free time and there are no new girls being admitted into the house. In fact, the doors have been shut for good. Ms. Terrance has said that there will be no more" God forsaken, good for nothing whores" in her house. This house, once full of fun and joy, has become cold and bitter.

I have been offered a job. A man, who frequents the inn across the street, has asked me to come keep his house in the woods. His name is Mr. Helding. He's an enormous man with gray eyes and although not very unsightly, he's somehow quite frightening. He offers to pay me fairly and says I may have all the books I'd like to read. In fact, he has even offered to buy my first three books. He says he will give them to me on Friday, the day I am to tell him if I accept his offer. As I am writing this well after midnight, sitting in the closet by the light of a nearly burned out candle, I think I will accept. I fear what Miss Terrance will do next, or worse yet, what I may do when I can no longer take her abuse.

Miss Terrance has warned me that,

if I take the job, I will be considered a disgrace to everyone who knows me. She says that my partnering with him will be sinful. He is a scoundrel, she says, and that I am not to leave. She says this as if I am her property! I have two days to make up my mind. I know nothing of Mr. Helding. Is he as bad as she makes him out to be? Would it be so sinful to work for a man with no wife or children without proper female guardianship? Perhaps. But it can only be better than living here under Ms. Terrance's cruel thumb. She is raising her niece to be just as deceitful, conniving and unloving as she is. I do not want to be any part of this darkened house. I believe I have just made up my mind. Now I must wait until Friday to inform Mr. Helding that I will come to him.

Flip. Running her hand along the page, Sarah flattened the paper. Daring a quick look at the video camera, she silently asked Shane the question and he shook his head. Nothing. Not even a flicker of paranormal activity. Sarah realized that she didn't think she could bear it if this experiment were to fail. If it did, then the Specters would be right, there would be no need to go on. Emily would be abandoned.

Looking around the room she could tell her friends were becoming bored. Todd yawned, wide and loud. Kate put down her pencil and leaned her head back against the wall. Only Shane still had fire in his eyes.

"Keep reading," Shane said.

"Mr. Helding has kept his word," she read on.

Today while I was in the front yard weeding, he approached me and gave me a brown paper-wrapped bundle. Inside was a copy of Heidi, a book of poetry and a very handsome volume about the original colonies. It was agreed that he would pick me up on Sunday, while everyone is at church. I've hidden my books carefully for I know what will happen if either of the two wicked women in this house finds them.

"There's a space here," Sarah said. "And the writing has changed, like she's scribbling. Listen to this."

I cannot stop the tears. Nor can I ease the pain from the bruise on my face. She has found my books. She gave her niece my copy of Heidi, and burned the poetry right in front of me. The other she threw at me, hitting me near my eye, all the while screaming hateful things at me. She accused me of doing sinful things with Mr. Helding. She called me horrid names and said that no decent man will ever marry me. Why does she do this? What have I done to her? Just a few more hours now before the sun comes up and then I will be gone. I'd rather have no husband at all, if that should be my fate, than to have to stay here one day more. Anywhere, even a house far from town will be a better place. At least, this is what I hope.

Chapter 18

"What time is it?" Sarah asked, rubbing her eyes.

"It's only eight-fifteen," Jamie answered.

"It feels like I've been reading forever," Sarah said as she stretched, sliding her long legs across the floor and flattening her back along the mattress.

"Are you up to reading a few more pages?" Shane asked.

"Are you sure you haven't caught anything?" she asked him.

"Not really, but we knew it might take some time. How are you guys doing over there? Dennis? Todd? Jamie?"

"Fine," they answered in unison.

Kate stood up and stretched, letting her pad and pencil fall to the floor.

"I know I'm not getting any vibes over here in my tiny corner of the world," she said.

"Come on, just a few more pages," Shane said. "We're up to the point where Farrell becomes involved. Once we start bringing him up, the energy has to pull at least one of them forward. If nothing happens by eleven o'clock, we'll stop, okay?"

"You want me to read for three more hours?" Sarah looked at him incredulously.

"Two hours and forty-five minutes if you start reading now," he said with a mischievous grin, his eyes sparkling.

"Hold on," Todd muttered. "Let me reload the camera."

Once the cameras were ready, and Kate sat back down, chewing on the end of her charcoal pencil, Sarah cleared her throat, nodded to the camcorder and began again.

The house is indeed deep in the woods. So far back I became lost after only a short distance. The road seemed to go on forever with nothing but thick fir trees on either side. The house is small, but very clean, and there are wonderful pines, maples and huge oaks surrounding the house. It's peaceful, like a kind of retreat. The fireplace is bigger than any I've ever seen and my room is just to the right of the living room. I have a comfortable bed, chest of drawers for my clothing and my window looks out across the back yard and to the wall of trees behind me.

Sarah paused to imagine Emily in this very room, looking out these very windows. She shivered and went on reading.

The quiet is intense. I swear I can hear the crickets snoring. I love it though. Mr. Helding, Farrell, as he demands to be called, cooked dinner tonight. He told me on how he likes his meals. Simple and well flavored, but nothing too fancy. I am to keep the house free of dirt, dust and critters. Do the laundry and tend to the gardens out back. I'll wash the dishes, of course. It's not that much to do, not after what I've been accustomed to doing. There's a clothesline out back. The stove is plenty big, and the pantry is well stocked. Farrell will pay for all things needed to keep the house. The money he gives me is for my clothing and what ever else I fancy.

The town is well over a mile or two from here, but the road leads right past the house so I should have no trouble walking to town. He warns, however, that I am never to go out so late in the afternoon that I'd end up traveling in the dark. And I am to never, ever, to go into the woods. He says they are not safe for a girl to wander about in.

Farrell works long hours, leaving with the sunrise and coming home long after it sets. I am to have his food hot and ready *on the table when I see him coming up the road. He says I am not to inquire about his day. His business is his own. After all of this he asked me when my birthday is. How curious. It just so happens that I will be seventeen in only three months. How quickly time goes by! It has been a year since I left the convent. He has given me permission to correspond with whomever I wish and he will mail the letters for me. I told him that I had written Sister Maria several times since coming to town, but have not received a reply. Farrell seemed rather, I don't know the right word, relieved, when I told him I have no other family.*

No family. How sad and lonely Emily must have felt. Sarah tried to swallow down the sorrow that constricted her throat, making it hard for her to breathe.

For the first time I believe I have seen a trace of the man I am working for. He came home very late tonight, stinking of whiskey. As he stumbled through the door, I first thought he was just stupidly drunk. But then I realized that blood was pouring from his nose and down his shirt! His left eye was swollen and turning a ghastly shade of black and blue. I ran to him immediately with a dish towel in hand but he shouted, " I am in no shape for a woman to be gawking at me!" I convinced him that he needed my help as I cleaned his face and put a cold compress on his eye while stripping him of his shirt so I could soak it and get as much blood out as possible. That was when he grabbed my hands very roughly and shoved me away." I don't need a woman's pampering," he growled. But I took his shirt anyway and left him. I hated seeing him covered in blood like that, with his eyes wild and cloudy. He is an incredibly strong man. When he pushed me backwards I nearly hit the floor.

Sarah looked up at Shane, frowning. Farrell couldn't be the murderer, yet his temper was so violent!

Four more times Farrell has come home covered in blood and stinking of whiskey. I have learned to keep my distance. I wanted to ask him the second time what shape the poor man he had scrapped with was in. The stone cold look on his face told me it was safer to hold my tongue. Each time he came home like this, he tossed me his shirt and I dutifully washed it. But I no longer try to tend his wounds. He doesn't seem to like me getting too close to him.

Today I turned seventeen. The summer heat is fading and the first touch of color has brought the trees to life. Farrell has not come home drunk in several days. Tonight he brought me a beautiful bouquet of daffodils and baby's breath. After dinner, he gave me another copy of Heidi. I can't believe he remembered what I had told him about Miss Terrance. And he has given me the day off tomorrow. Also, I have extra money, a second gift, to buy myself something nice in town. I know just the store I want to stop in! I will buy some silk and sweet smelling soaps and maybe a bottle of perfume.

Farrell is a strange man. I see two men inside that grizzly bear of a body, one is harsh, troubled and cold, the other is seemingly shy and sensitive. Sometimes I have strange thoughts that I don't dare repeat, even here. I suppose it is because I am a woman now. I believe Farrell knows, too.

Sarah looked up.

"It's very confusing not having any kind of date or time to follow," she said.

"Well we know she's been with him three months at least," Kate said, scribbling on her pad.

"What are you drawing?" Sarah asked.

"Look." Kate turned the pad around so they could all see. A young woman stood, neatly drawn and shaded, looking out the open window, open to a lawn that spread out like a blanket. Beyond it, great dark pines reached to the heavens.

"I'm not sure what she looks like," Kate said. "That's why I drew her looking out the window."

As if pulled by invisible strings, they all turned and looked at the dark window. Sarah was the first to turn away.

"This isn't going anywhere," she mumbled.

And it was true. She had been reading for over two hours and nothing had come of it. Although what she had read was interesting, but what had they learned? Only that Farrell had mood swings, and that Emily was happy and that she was no longer a girl. Sure, Emily had let them know that Farrell had a dark side, particularly when drunk, and that he was a troubled man. But a monster? Also, he didn't seem to be as fearsome as her dreams had portrayed him. This fact alone puzzled her. How could his reputation have been so bad if there had not been something on which to base it?

She shrugged her shoulders. Everyone except Shane was getting weary, hungry and cramped, mainly because he had made it very clear in the beginning that no one was to move or make a sound while the reading was going on. If the diary was going to conjure up Emily's spirit he wanted to catch every bit of it without interference. He had also made it clear that he did not want to risk the chance of a cough, a sigh or even a twitch of a finger losing the connection with the dead.

"How about a dinner break?" Sarah asked.

"Oh please," Todd begged, grabbing his stomach and pretending to be starving.

"We have plenty of time to come back," Sarah added.

Shane turned off the camcorder. "Fine," he said moodily.

The air in the kitchen was strained and quiet as they helped themselves to leftovers and sandwiches. Everyone seemed afraid to speak until Jamie finally broke the silence.

"Kind of disappointing, isn't it?" she said. "I mean, the diary isn't revealing any nitty-gritty details. It's just the diary of a young woman whose life was less than exciting. She lived in a different world, sure. But other than Farrell's blood thirst for the fist fight, nothing dramatic is happening."

"But we haven't gotten to the point where the sheriff comes in yet," Sarah reminded her, hiding her own disappointment. "We're still in the introduction phase."

"Maybe he doesn't," Kate said.

"What do you mean?" Sarah asked.

"Maybe he doesn't come into play other than the fact that he saw her dead body. How do we know he was involved at all? He's not the sicko that killed her."

Kate pushed her plate away, leaving a sandwich half eaten and Sarah knew that she was upset, too.

"That's not true," she argued. "I know it. Well, I know he plays a prominent role. Someone else does, anyway. Remember the stranger? We need to find out about him."

"How do you know?" Dennis asked.

"The same way I've known anything so far," Sarah told him. "I just feel it. It's as if Emily is somewhere inside my head, telling me things. Like she's slipped in here and is blending her thoughts with my own. Don't look at me as if I am insane, Dennis. I don't care what you think anymore. I know something happened. And I know that something is happening to me and I can't explain it." She stood up and turned her back to them. A strange ocean of emotions had begun swelling inside her again, she suddenly wanted to cry.

Shane finished his sandwich and stood up, too. Giving Dennis a dark look, he led the way back to Sarah's bedroom.

"Hey, I thought I turned this off," Todd said looking over at his camera, which faced the door. Just as Sarah entered the room, it set off a series of shots. Click, click, click. Then it shut off, the red glowing eye fading as the camera died.

They stood there, staring at the camera in disbelief.

"I know I had turned this off," Todd repeated.

"Well, Jamie," Shane said, rushing over to his video equipment. "I think your disappointment has come to a crashing halt."

"Dennis, you saw me turn it off, right?" Todd persisted.

"Yeah, I did," Dennis answered, checking his camera.

"Do you think Emily turned it back on?" Jamie asked, excited.

"Or Farrell," Sarah said. "Don't forget we have two ghosts here." As an afterthought she added, "One may want the truth more than the other."

"What?" Five voices asked as one.

"Think about it!" Sarah told them. "Emily knows who killed her. She knows how she felt and about whom. Think! Who is the one person that never lived to find out the truth, who died in the dark thinking he had been betrayed?"

"Farrell," they answered.

"Exactly! Maybe we've been expecting the wrong ghost to show up."

Sarah's emotions were going haywire. She jumped up and

down in her excitement. She was getting closer. She could feel it. Then the full impact of what might be happening struck her and she grew very still.

"He frightens you, doesn't he?" Shane asked her.

"He's angry," Sarah replied. "He may not have been so bad in life, but I swear, in death, he's a raging bull."

"Well, let's see what else Emily can tell us," Shane said, flipping the power switch on the camera.

As he put his eye against the viewfinder, he let out a gasp. He lowered his face again, holding his breath.

"Holy shhh-!" he exclaimed. "Come here, Sarah, and look at this."

Instead of having a clear view of the bed with no one sitting on it, Sarah saw a large dark shape sunk deep into the mattress. The form was definitely that of a man, and somehow, he seemed to give the impression of waiting.

"Farrell," Sarah said softly.

"Go back and start reading," Shane said.

Sarah looked through the viewfinder again, she could no longer see Farrell. But he *had* been there, sitting on the edge of her bed, looking right at her. She felt as though she were covered in ice, every part of her tingled.

Was he aware of them? Could he see the cameras and did he *know* what they were doing? These thoughts pulsed through her mind, creating a rhythmic throb.

"What's going on?" Todd asked.

"Nothing. I'm just adjusting things," Shane told him.

Sarah shook her head, but he gave her a gentle shove

towards the bed.

"You have to continue," he said.

Somehow, she managed to seat herself back down on the bed. She sat opposite the spot where she had seen Farrell's dark form. With the throbbing tempo still playing against her skull, she picked up the diary.

Just as she turned the page, a cold, dry touch caressed her hand.

Chapter 19

The feeling that raced through Sarah was beyond fear. At first, when she began to read, her tongue tripped over the words.

I've never felt such mixed emotions before. I know it's been quite some time since I last wrote. I guess it is because I have been afraid of what I might admit. For about three weeks now Sheriff Edmond Brewler has been frequenting the house while Farrell is off working. Of course, he says that he is just doing his lawful duty, making sure the woman of the house is safe. Of course I am. What could harm me way out here? But he doesn't seem to be convinced. I wonder if he has other reasons for coming. I can't be sure, but I could swear sometimes I believe this. He's a very attractive man, tall and strong. Not so big as Farrell, yet manly nevertheless with the brightest blue eyes I've ever seen. How they sparkle!

Last Sunday while I was in town, he stopped me on the street and asked me to consider an offer. He wants me to care for his two children and be his housekeeper, as well. It seems his wife is ill and cannot do chores these days because she tires so easily. And more days than not, she is in bed with headaches and stomach pains. He offers to pay me more than what I am making now. A part of me would love to take his offer. His house is enormous, with gardens and large green lawns. However, another part of me feels like I will be betraying Farrell. In a time when I thought my life was nothing but despair, he saved me. He offered me a way to be on my own, without any commitments. And Farrell has never given any signs of personal interest in me. He keeps a respectable distance. Sometimes this annoys me, as funny as that may sound.

I wish I had more time to spend in town, to socialize with other girls my age. Perhaps if I took the job at the Sheriff's house I could build up a good reputation for myself and earn friends. Yet, still it nags me that it's wrong, that the Sheriff has other interests. He's a married man! Oh but he is so handsome, charming and intelligent! The funniest thought came to me. What if he is looking to replace his wife? And I am his target? And if she was to die, would that be so wrong?

Last night I tried to flirt a little with Farrell, just to see if I could get a reaction from him, to see if I am appealing to him. I know it is silly, but I needed to know. All he did was stare at me, all quiet, and after a few minutes he simply got up, put his hat on and walked out of the house! I guess that was answer enough!

Sarah felt a pang of anger at Farrell's rejection. Emily must have been beautiful. What was wrong with him?

The sheriff stopped by yet again today. He brought me a pie his wife made. It drained her of all her energy, but, he said, she was in the baking mood. She seems pleased at the idea of me coming to help her with the children and chores. Just when I thought his visit would be quick, he turned to me and said, "Emily, you're all cooped up here. Come and walk with me a little. I know a path not far from this house. Oh, I know these woods better than anyone, including Farrell. I grew up here, you know. Come on, the walk will do you some good." Then he led me out the back door and into the woods.

I was more than nervous, my stomach was full of all sorts of butterflies. But I let him lead me to a path that was nothing but a narrow strip of dirt parting some pine trees. Funny as it may be, the path brought us out to a small and very old cemetery that hasn't been tended to for years by the looks of the long grass. The tombstones are delicately carved, even though their inscriptions are faded. There was a lovely peacefulness about the place, and a big oak tree. We sat under the tree, chewing on some fresh jerky and talked about nothing serious. He told me that his house was just on the other side of the cemetery. Before I knew it, the light was fading and Farrell would be home soon.

Pausing for breath, Sarah thought how strange it was that she could see the place Emily was describing so clearly, almost as though she had been there with her. She continued reading, wanting to know more.

The Sheriff walked me back home and left. The day didn't end there, however. I

had my first true argument with Farrell
that night. Apparently he had come home
early and found me missing. And he was
in a rage! I decided to keep the truth of
where I was to myself, and simply said I
had taken a walk.

"The woods are no place for a woman!"
he hollered at me. His voice shook, his
hands clenched into fists and his face
turned a horrid shade of red. "Don't you
know the things that can happen to a
woman?" Then he came at me so fast
and grabbed me by the arm. I thought
for a moment he was going to strike me,
but then I saw this funny look on his
face like he was more hurt than angry.
He slammed out of house, staying on
the porch for a long time, muttering to
himself. I haven't dared used the path
since.

Farrell had grabbed her, forcefully! He *did* have the temper
Mr. Brewler told them about. But, Sarah thought, he hadn't
hurt Emily. He walked away.

I couldn't help myself! The solitude of
this house got to me these past nine days.
Spring is fully upon us with all its sweet
smells and ripe color. I could not help
but wander! My feet itched to walk that
path again. I found it easy enough, and let
it lead me back to the cemetery.

This time, there was an eerie feel about the cemetery. Perhaps it was because I was there alone. Once I stepped off the path and into the opening, it felt as if I left the real world behind. I had brought a book with me so I sat by that tree and read for a while. Then I walked around a bit, reading the old headstones. There is this one pillar that's like a tall marble tower, with a tip like a pyramid. I stood there, running my hands over the marble and suddenly the Sheriff was right there beside me!

"Lovely, isn't it?" he said to me. "Legend has it that a woman is buried there. But the husband wanted her to be left in peace, with no more ties to this world, so he refused to put her name in stone."

Then he scolded me for walking about alone. Like Farrell, he warned me of how the woods are no place for a woman. Then he offered to escort me back. He seemed different this time. While we were still in the trees, he grabbed me and kissed me full on the lips! My knees went weak and I stumbled, falling into him. He wrapped me in his arms and I felt like I couldn't breathe.

The Sheriff was her secret lover! Sarah laughed out loud. She knew it.

It was a very awkward evening with Farrell. I felt so guilty. I just knew he could see the Sheriff's lip prints on my own. And my cheeks! I couldn't stop blushing! Farrell looked at me queerly from time to time, but never said a word. While I was cleaning the kitchen, he disappeared. Later, as I was crawling into bed, I found the sweetest little poem lying upon my pillow. I am keeping it tucked inside my diary.

"The poem's gone," Sarah said frowning as she flipped through the pages.

"It would have been nice to have it, but it's not as important. Keep reading," Shane said impatiently.

Sarah could see by the look on his face that he was catching something on camera.

Chapter 20

A sudden pain ricocheted across her forehead bouncing from temple to temple. As she tried to continue reading, her voice caught in her throat. Fear, like none she had ever known, pulsed through her but she needed to go on. She had to.

I'm scared. The Sheriff told me that he would not lose to a man like Farrell. This time when he kissed me, he bruised my lips. They are still swollen and tender. And he gripped me so hard I have rings of brownish-yellow around my upper arms. What's worse, Farrell noticed, calling me all sorts of horrible names. He ranted on and on about how he had warned the Sheriff to stay away from his property. Yelling that I was encouraging the Sheriff. I couldn't deny anything, and this seemed to hurt him. It seemed as though he was waiting for me to fight back and swear I'd never done such things. Finally, he told me that I am never to go near Sheriff Brewler again. Ever, or else there would be hell to pay.

Sarah thought about the words "hell to pay". She could practically hear him warning her. Maybe he did kill Emily. *No! I can't give up on him yet.* There was only one way to find out. Sarah kept going.

I want to leave. Just slip away into the shadows and rid these two men and myself the trouble I have caused. I do not wish to hurt either one of them. But I feel for both!

Suddenly, a gust of icy wind swept through the room, knocking the diary out of Sarah's hands and to the floor where it landed with a hard thud, the pages fluttering like mad. Then, just as fast as it happened, it was over.

"Holy cow!" Jamie breathed.

The lights flickered, and the cameras whined in protest. The camcorder stopped and started then stopped again. Something powerful was among them.

When Sarah jumped up off the bed, her foot caught on something hard and the voice recorder, completely forgotten, shot out from beneath the dust ruffle of her bed and slid across the floor. At the very instant Sarah bent down to pick it up, the red record button popped. Startled, she jumped back, then, picking it up, rewound the tape and pressed play. Her voice filled the room, reiterating Emily's private conversations with herself. She placed her thumb over the stop button then froze.

Rewinding the tape just a bit, she hit play and turned up the volume all the way. Again her voice spilled forth. This time, however there was something different. It sounded like... No, that couldn't be. Sarah listened harder, putting her ear up against the recorder. Yes, she could hear it. There were two voices reading, in perfect unison, hers and another softer voice. Then, in the silence that designated the time during which they had all gone to the kitchen, another sound was captured.

This time Emily's voice filled the room as she spoke words of promise and love and soon they could hear her sobbing. When Sarah began reading the part of Farrell and his warning and Emily's confession of love for both men, there came yet another sound.

It was the all too familiar voice that Sarah had come to fear. It was only a whisper, but it was enough to send the coldest of chills running up her spine.

"Emily," Farrell cried in a heartbroken plea.

Sarah turned off the tape and sat down. She looked over at Shane. His face was flushed.

"Did you get much?" she asked, remembering what she'd seen when they had returned.

Without a smile, frown or any sign showing on his face, he simply stated, "I've been getting non stop footage since we came back."

Shane hooked up the camcorder to the bedroom television.

"You sure?" he asked, before beginning to play back the tape.

"Yes," she said.

As the screen lit up, they all gasped in disbelief, because Sarah was not alone on the bed.

"Dear God!" Dennis exclaimed, his eyes glued to the set.

There were three people sitting on that bed, first Sarah, her image clear and sharp and beside her an enormous grayish shadow that was Farrell. Behind her, sitting very close was Emily, her shoulders shaking as though she were weeping.

What the video also revealed was the reason for the diary's sudden plummet to the floor. In an apparent fit of rage, Farrell stood up and swiped the diary out of Sarah's hand. Then he stormed out of the room, creating the wind that had flapped the pages. Emily looked up then, and put a hand on Sarah's shoulder.

Not only had they both been present, each one had touched her! Sarah shivered, wiping her clammy hands down her thighs. She did it! She brought back not one, but two ghosts.

"Did you see how clearly we could see them?" Todd said. "Sure they broke up now and then. But they were there, so real."

"She touched your shoulder, Sarah," Jamie said.

"I know," Sarah said. When Farrell had touched her, it had been cold. When Emily touched her, the headache disappeared. What did it all mean?

"We need some fresh air," Shane said, turning off the TV.

Outside, pacing back and forth, they debated whether Emily's ghost was aware of Farrell and vice versa. The thought of it hung in the air like a spring fog. Oh what a ripple that would cause in the world of spiritual and paranormal research! If it could be proven that ghosts had conscious awareness, it would open a whole new field to be investigated. And now, it appeared, they had two very ripe ghosts to help them find some of those answers.

Sarah rubbed her temples. The nagging headache was determined to come back. It crept up her neck, along her jaw, and around her ears until it rested in the hollow pits of her temples. She snapped her fingers to catch everyone's attention.

"I should keep reading," she said, "Do we have tape left?"

"Absolutely," Shane replied with an excited smile.

Once they were back in Sarah's bedroom, it was clear that no one felt as comfortable as before, Jamie and Kate scanned every nook and corner with frightened eyes. As for Sarah, she took a rather long time deciding where to sit, recalling the image of Farrell so very close to her. Was he there now, watching and waiting? And Emily. Was she still there? And were her tears still falling?

It was all happening too fast. The pain intensified, doubling her over. Did all psychics and mediums feel such discomfort? Was it some kind of psychic pressure? Whatever it was, it was almost too much to bear.

Sitting on the edge of the bed, she opened the diary, the spine of the book was beginning to crack apart, revealing the yellowed glue beneath the yellowed pages. Carefully, she thumbed nearly two-thirds of the way through without bothering to look at the camera. She could hear Dennis and

Todd resetting the automatic timers on theirs and she knew Shane was aleady one step ahead of her as though he had his own psychic power.

Inhaling deeply, she allowed the breath to fill her all the way down to her toes. Letting the breath out slow and measured, she began to read again.

Farrell continued to watch me like a hawk. I never know when he is going to come home. Twice I have caught him prowling about while hanging out the laundry or weeding the garden. If I should happen not to be in sight when he comes home, he bellows his bloody head off until I come running, scared to death.

Worst of all, he is drinking so much. When he does come home he reeks of it. His eyes are red and watery all of the time now. I have tried to talk with him. But everything I say seems to come out wrong. I've sent him into some mighty fine rants so I have decided to just keep my mouth shut and let him work it out for himself.

Was this where things went wrong? A nasty temper never mixes well with liquor. As bad as she felt, Sarah couldn't stop questioning Farrell. Everything so far pointed right at him.

I have neither seen nor heard from the Sheriff. I admit that I do not really miss him. His last visit shook me so much. I am more worried about Farrell. I guess that tells me where my heart truly lies.

However, I cannot stop the wild dreams. In each one the Sheriff comes and takes me away to a place of great beauty, giving me everything I have ever dreamed of having and loving me passionately. Ah. It is well past midnight and I must sleep or I will be no good in the morning to do my chores.

I went to town today. Much to my excitement and despair, the Sheriff caught up with me. He asked me to come have lunch at his house. He said it was a formal offer of employment and that his wife wants to meet me. He seemed very cool and indifferent. He simply wants me to meet his family. Before I could stop myself, I had agreed. A small light lit behind his eyes and he whispered that he knows for a fact that Farrell will be out of town all of tomorrow, and I needn't be afraid. Sheriff Brewler seems to be under the impression that I am terrified of Farrell and that he has abused me.

Why would the Sheriff think that? Sarah wondered, trying to place herself in his shoes. Farrell was a big, mean-tempered man, this was all very apparent. Yet, Emily had not once mentioned him hitting her, just the one time when she thought he would.

Today is the day that I will go and meet the Brewlers. Farrell has said that he shouldn't be home until very late and stated very coldly that I am to have the house in perfect shape when he returns. As he spoke to me, his eyes shimmered with what looked like red-hot anger, as if he knows I am up to something.

Again that anger! Had Farrell never expressed anything else?

It has been an exhausting day, emotionally. Thrilling to say the least, too. I made it to the Sheriff's. I have never seen such beauty! Rose gardens and pebbled paths with water fountains in the front yard! His wife is beautiful, as are his children. His oldest, Little Edmond, is sixteen and is a mirror image of his father. It was really very remarkable to see them side-by-side. Though, I must say that Little Edmond worried me. He followed me everywhere, always at my heels. And the way he stared at me, it gave me chills!

Oh I cannot describe how confused I am! My heart yearns for the open beauty of what the Sheriff's home offers. But I feel at home here. I have spent so much time and energy here. My heart is torn between the two houses as much as for the men who own them.

Sarah closed the book.

"I can't read anymore," she said, rubbing her eyes. The

others agreed that they were exhausted. Even Shane was ready to call it a night. It was, Sarah thought, as much emotional as physical exhaustion. After all, they had seen and heard things tonight that they had never dreamed of.

Half an hour later all of the equipment was packed and everyone but Sarah and Jamie were heading for the front door.

"That was truly incredible," Shane said, his hand on the knob.

"I still can't believe it's all happening," Sarah replied.

"Me too." Jamie said. "But let's talk about it tomorrow afternoon, late afternoon. I'm exhausted."

"Are we sleeping in your room?" Jamie asked once the house was quiet.

"There's nowhere else," Sarah said. "You know that, but don't worry. They're gone."

"How can you be sure?" Jamie demanded.

"I can feel Emily when she's around," Sarah explained. "Farrell, too. Believe me, right now the house is empty. Come on, let's get some sleep."

Back in the room, they settled in for what was left of the night. As Sarah lay with her hands folded beneath her head, she seemed to hear Emily reading from the diary. Was it Emily's voice, she wondered, or her own? Or were they one in the same?

Chapter 21

Sarah wasn't sure if she was awake or not. A strange feeling, cool and wet, crept up her legs starting at her ankles and winding its way up to her knees. She tried to open her eyes but found she couldn't. Leaden weights seemed to seal her eyes shut and the same weights pulled her down until, all of a sudden, she seemed to soar upwards. Riding waves of unconsciousness, she drifted between sleep and awareness.

Sarah inhaled deeply trying to regain control over her mind and body. Exerting every bit of willpower she could conjure up, she forced herself out of the strong grip of slumber. The milky glow of the moon washed over her in pale puddles and she could hear crickets chirping. She held her breath, as she heard the unmistakable sound of a man snoring!

When Sarah opened her eyes at last, she knew immediately that she wasn't Sarah anymore. The sheets felt rough to the touch and when she had fallen asleep, she had been dressed in her silk Mickey Mouse boxers and a cotton tank top. Now she was wearing a cotton nightgown cut high at the neck.

Emily, Sarah thought. I'm Emily.

All she could see was a deep gray mist, that swept in silent currents, like rain, shifting, spiraling down, sweeping across the floor like a moving carpet.

She didn't belong here. That was what the mist was telling her. It was pushing her away.

"Don't go any further," it hissed.

"Why not?" she asked.

"Don't go any further," the mist repeated.

Looking back, she saw a faint light shining pink and warm and inviting. It wavered in the distance beyond reach yet reachable, if she only chose to go back.

"Go back," the mist repeated.

Sarah looked into the vast void opening up before her, a void filled with mist. And she was caught in it, inside of Here, There and NoWhere.

"What if I go forward?" she asked.

"Don't go any further," the mist insisted.

"But I must!" Sarah said.

Suddenly, she was pushed forward into the nothingness, away from the safety of her own self, her own world.

But wait! Now the nothing had turned into something. But

it was the kind of something she had no right to know, the truth of a dark time when blood pooled in the grass of an old cemetery.

She had, she knew, reached the doorway between two worlds. Two young women had found each other and now they needed one another in a bizarre way.

Was this insanity? Or did she have power over her reality, a power that allowed her to see the past as well as the present?

When she took a step forward, the path closed in behind her. Another step. And now the mist was pushing frantically against her. Only this time it was urging her on. No longer did it whisper warnings. Now she was moving forward, quickly, endlessly until finally the mist rose and became a cloud, hovering above tall grass and spindly weeds.

She was in a familiar place. The cemetery stretched out before her and she found herself before a marble monument, its surface smooth, untouched by words.

"Isn't it beautiful?" a man said and, spinning around, she saw a handsome face, a dazzling smile.

"Mr. Brewler," she exclaimed. "What are you doing here?"

The man stared down at her, clearly confused, running a hand through his silvering hair. His blue eyes were mesmerizing in their clarity. And he was incredibly handsome, from the cut of his jaw to the arch of his brow. Age had weathered him graciously. Instead of taking from him, the years gave him a striking quality of wisdom and something else, something she couldn't quite identify.

Sarah smiled. She couldn't help herself. He had a magic about him that just stole all common sense away.

"Does Farrell know you're here?" he asked her.

Sarah raised an eyebrow. Farrell?

"Does he, Emily?" he insisted.

Oh no. Sarah was herself inside, but to him, she was Emily. And this man wasn't Mr. Brewler, the man she had met. He was Sheriff Brewler! Suddenly, she was very, very frightened. She had to say something. But what?

"No, he doesn't," she said. She had no idea whether he did or not but it was all she could think to say.

"Good. I want to talk to you," the Sheriff said. "Why are you flinching like that? I'm not going to hurt you."

She hadn't realized she had flinched when he reached forward to push a stray lock of hair behind her ear.

"He's been hitting you, hasn't he?" he demanded.

"He doesn't hit me," Sarah protested. "He never has."

"Don't protect him," he said. "Why won't you accept my offer?"

Sarah thought fast. The diary. Think now, what had she read in it that would give her a clue as to what to say?

"It doesn't seem right. I just can't. I mean -" she stopped. She didn't know *what* she meant.

"My wife knows she's dying," he told her. "She wants me to be happy. She wants the children to be well cared for, and they adore you. My daughter giggled for hours after you left the other day, talking about how pretty you are, how sweet. And Edmond, he seemed so calm and at peace when he was with you. I've never seen him so subdued. Please, Emily. I am begging you. Annie needs you to take her place in the house. The children are going to need a mother and I need you."

He took her face in his hands. His eyes were tender. Sarah backed away from him and found herself pressed against the marble monument.

"Don't be afraid of me. Why are you so afraid of me?" he demanded.

"It's not right," she whispered.

"What isn't?" he asked.

"Replacing your wife," Sarah said. Her mind was spinning too fast. She felt dizzy and sick to her stomach. "She's not even dead yet and already you kiss me and ask me to come live with you."

A hot flash of anger crossed his face.

"What's the matter with you?" he said. "We've been through this."

They had? Oh, she didn't know enough! There was no way Emily could have written everything down. And she didn't have Emily's thoughts or memories.

"How long do you think she has?" Sarah asked.

"A few more months, maybe. Doc says her heart is failing. Why?" He eyed her suspiciously.

She couldn't answer. A few months! What kind of turmoil Emily must have lived through. She could not even imagine what Emily had felt. The emotional struggle she must have fought.

"I'm offering you a better life," he said. "Farrell is a drunk and a vile, violent man. I see it when you don't. I see the mess he makes of the men in town when he's in a rage. He'll end up killing you. You have to come with me, Emily. I can protect you, love you, give you anything you could want. We all love you. Why can't you see that? Farrell doesn't love you. He can't love anything. Don't you want to be loved?"

Her feelings were no longer her own. She was, she realized, completely in Emily's thrall now. And how she wanted to be loved! Tears slipped past her long dark lashes and slid down her cheeks. She could feel the ache in Emily's heart, as if it were her own. In a voice that had been Emily's true voice she looked square into the Sheriff's eyes.

"Yes," she whispered.

Sheriff Brewler lowered his face to hers. But before his lips could touch her own, everything disappeared.

Sarah stood in the mist alone.

"No more!" the mist hissed at her. And then it abandoned her so suddenly she felt naked and vulnerable. In that moment, she realized that the mist had been Emily's energy, her spirit. She wanted Sarah to see, to feel what it was she had lived through. But, in the end, it had been too much for her to bear.

When Sarah next opened her eyes, she found herself lying in her bed, where she belonged. And the diary, opened to a page, was lying on the pillow beside her, although she knew for a fact that she had placed it on the dresser by the alarm clock before she and Jamie had gone to bed. It was just light enough outside that she could read the page.

The Sheriff confessed his love for me. Out of the corner of my eye I saw someone standing behind the trees watching us.

Sarah dropped the book.

"Oh my God," she whispered.

Careful not to wake Jamie, Sarah slipped out of bed and went to the window. Looking out into the early morning dimness, her heart flip-flopped when she saw that her back yard was completely blanketed by a fine gray mist that swirled across the ground like a moving carpet.

Chapter 22

"Sarah! Wake up!" Jamie urged, pushing on her shoulder.

"What?" she asked, trying to shake the fog out of her mind. Her body felt like lead. She couldn't remember getting back into bed, let alone closing her eyes and falling asleep. At least it had been a good sound sleep with no more dreams.

"Come on, get up. You are not going to believe this!" Jamie said, bouncing up and down on the edge of the bed.

"Shane called," Jamie continued, throwing the blankets off the bed. "He was up all night developing the film from the cameras last night, and he got some serious stuff. Remember how in the video Emily and Farrell were sitting on the bed? Well! On the prints, it shows them everywhere! They're all over the room. But they never moved in the video! Isn't that just too cool? They're all on their way over now. Kate can't come because her mom is making her go to her aunt's house. Hurry up, get dressed!"

Sarah's mind buzzed. The foggy feeling refused to lift and it was hard to concentrate on Jamie. Her friend's high-pitched voice resonated clearly, yet the words themselves muddled together. Sarah tried to think. Photos. Emily and Farrell in her room, when? Emily! Sarah jumped out of bed, grabbing a pair of jeans. Now she remembered.

"Wait until I tell you guys what happened to me last night," Sarah said while she slid into the jeans and tossed a boy band T-shirt over her head. Adrenaline shot right to her head and found the new tender spots on either side. Ignoring the pain, she grabbed up her hair and tied a Scruncii around it.

"What?" Jamie said, frowning. "I was here all night and nothing happened."

"Something did, though," Sarah said. "It was awesome and scary. Just wait."

By the time they reached the kitchen, the phone was ringing. Sarah snatched it up.

"Hello? Oh hey. Okay no problem," she hung up. "That was Shane, they're stuck in traffic, some kind of accident on the highway. They'll be here as soon as they can."

"So you're going to tell me first, right?" Jamie asked, pouring a bowl of Cheerios.

"No, I'm not," Sarah answered. "You'll have to wait."

"Oh come off it!" Jamie pleaded.

Sarah had known Jamie would refuse to be put off. And

Sarah couldn't deny she was busting at the seams to tell her.

So she told Jamie about the incredible dream and the mist, about waking up to find the diary on her pillow, about what she had read and the fog outside her window. Jamie just sat there, her mouth hanging open.

"Jamie, you have milk dripping down your chin," Sarah said, laughing. Somehow just talking about what had happened eased her headache. Now she saw that the important thing was that Emily was communicating directly with her. She knew, without a doubt, Emily wanted them to find out who had murdered her.

"Let's read some more," Jamie said.

"No, we can't," Sarah said. "Not without the others."

It felt wrong to even think about revealing more of the past until they were all together. What would they do if Emily and Farrell materialized again and they had no equipment to catch it?

"Please!" Jamie begged.

Sarah couldn't resist those big brown puppy-dog eyes.

"Fine," she said, "but just a few pages, no more."

They settled in the living room, the morning light pouring through the bay windows. It was warm and inviting but they both sat huddled together.

Sarah opened the diary and flipped past the pages she'd already read until she found the passage she had read that morning and realized that it was written two full pages after the point where she'd stopped reading. Had she read more while Jamie slept and not even known it? Is that how the diary had come to be on her pillow? She backtracked and started reading.

I've gone to the Brewler's on two more occasions. I do not know what is wrong with me. I know I should stay far away from him and his family. But I can't! He is so handsome and charming.

Today Little Edmond – how can I call him little when he is a full foot taller than me – gave me a bunch of flowers he had picked from their garden, even though he gave me a fright, suddenly appearing in the back yard, so quiet. Just like his father. And he is just like his father in so many ways. I swear I saw a wicked gleam in his eyes when I nearly screamed. Oh, and he has his father's crystal eyes!

Sheriff Brewler told me that he hopes to have more children. "Do you want children?" he asked me. I told him I had never given it much thought. Then the strangest thing happened. That night over dinner, Farrell asked me if I planned on having children! He was in quite a sour mood and sulked all night. He sat with me only long enough to finish his plate of stew and then left. When he came home way after midnight, he went stumbling through the house, cursing. He came to my room and stood outside the door. As I pretended to sleep, my skin crawled along my arms and neck.

Sarah turned the page. She thought for a moment about how odd it was that both men would ask her about children in the same day. Did Farrell truly know what Emily was doing? Maybe he was spying on them. And maybe, with his drunken behavior and rage, he really did kill Emily. Once again, she began to doubt Farrell. A pang of emotion tightened her stomach. She kept reading.

Today I decided I needed a moment or two to think and so I forgot about my chores and went walking around the cemetery. Just a few days ago, Farrell asked if I want children, and now he asked if I am comfortable. I wish I could read his mind sometimes, just to help me figure out what he is thinking. He has grown gray around the eyes, as if he's sick. I think it is the alcohol that is doing him in. He's always drunk these days. I lied to him and told him I was just happy here.

But I am not. I am so bored. I figured this out while I was walking around the cemetery, keeping company with the dead. I am bored down to my very soul. I hate doing nothing but cleaning and cooking and walking around graves! I feel so trapped here.

A few times I stole through the woods and across the cemetery and made my way to the Sheriff's. There, I feel alive and ashamed but young again.

Young! Just writing the word makes me laugh. I am only seventeen and I feel like an old maid already. It is getting harder and harder to refuse the Sheriff's constant offer.

I have such mixed emotions about Farrell. At times I hate him and his bullish behavior. But then I feel something stir deep inside me. And that is when I begin to feel guilty for even thinking of leaving. It's so strange. I am afraid of him yet drawn to him, often at the same time. And then there is the Sheriff. I can't seem to bring myself to call him by his name, I don't know why. Yet, I feel something so very intense in my heart for him and our kisses are getting more and more passionate.

Then there is Annie Brewler. She is getting weaker by the day. The doctor is frequenting the house almost daily, the Sheriff tells me. I can't stop the horrible thoughts that creep into my head. I daydream of being the lady of the house with a maid of my own and of having the freedom to go where I wish, do what I wish. But to think that I can have these things only at the expense of another woman's life!

Wow, Sarah thought, the stress Emily must have been

under! So many emotions all colliding together must have been horrible to bear. She couldn't begin to imagine what it would have felt like, with all that on the conscience.

> *Once again the Sheriff met me in the cemetery. I saw him coming this time and surprised myself at how boldly I approached him. I even allowed him to take my hand as we were standing by the marble monument. He said it was beautiful and then he said that I was, too.*

Sarah stopped reading and let the book fall to the floor.

"Are you all right?" Jamie asked. "You're as white as a sheet!"

Sarah knew what was coming next. But she needed to know for sure. Picking up the journal, she read, and as she did, she remembered her dream in all its vividness.

> *He asked me if Farrell knew where I was and I told him that of course he didn't. Then he demanded to know if Farrell had been hitting me. I swore he was not and never has. But the Sheriff didn't believe me. He went on rambling about how much more he can offer me. How he is a better man than Farrell.*

> *"Don't you want to be loved?" he asked me. This is when I started crying. The tears just came and I couldn't stop them. I cried on his shoulder for what seemed like forever. All the while he held me, his face in my hair. It felt so good! After a while, I looked him in the face and told*

him yes, I did want to be loved. And I do! So much so! That was when he kissed me over and over again and told me that he loved me, too.

Sarah closed her eyes. She did not need to see the words to know what happened next.

"I saw someone out of the corner of my eye," she said. "Standing behind a tree, watching us."

"You mean that someone was watching Emily," Jamie said. "Stop it, Sarah! You're scaring me."

Sarah saw the relief in her friend's eyes as she heard the doorbell ring and she saw how fast Jamie hurried to let the others in.

Jamie must have thought that, for a moment, Sarah actually thought she was the girl who had, so long ago, lived and loved in this very house.

And it was true.

For a moment, Sarah really *had* felt as though she was Emily.

Chapter 23

Everyone wanted to talk first. Jamie, always the loudest, went on and on about what Sarah had just read to her. It seemed, Sarah thought, that it was easier for Jamie to accept it if she told it. Not once did Jamie meet her gaze, and she failed to mention the part where Sarah had seemed to confuse herself with Emily.

"By the way, where's all of your equipment?" she asked.

"I decided not to bring it today," Shane said. "We need to go over the photos and discuss what it all means. I'm sorry, but today needs to be a ghost day."

"A ghost day?" Sarah said.

"Yes, a ghost day," Shane explained "We need to set the mystery part aside for now and focus on the evidence of the paranormal activity we have here. Have you thought about that? We possibly have the first real hard evidence of the existence of ghosts in our hands. We discovered them, we caught them on film, we can even conjure them up. We have film, video, EVP's. We have it all! What we need now is to study the evidence and determine exactly what we have and what we're going to do with it. We can take this to a whole new level."

He was right. Sarah knew that. But that did nothing to dull the ache in her heart. Never having believed before, she was now wide awake to the possibilities of the paranormal and she understood why so many, including Shane, were obsessed with it. For one reason, the concept of life beyond the body went beyond human comprehension. It bent the rules. However, this was still about Emily.

Emily was more than a ghost. She was a real person with emotions and love and fear, dead but not entirely gone. For whatever reasons, she lived on and had come to Sarah and opened up her world to her. But why her? Why not Jamie with all of her exuberance? Why not Shane for that matter? Wouldn't he be a better host? He's intelligent, far more experienced. He believed with body and soul in ghosts. That was what should matter above all else. However, Emily had chosen her to do something that she had not been able to do herself in life. And it was a grave responsibility.

Given all that, Sarah knew she couldn't just look at Emily as an apparition, as nothing more than a disembodied ghost with no voice, no soul. Emily was more than a trapped spirit. She couldn't just toss it all to the side.

But the others didn't seem to understand this. Their ideas were about the excitement of being famous, being guests on talk shows, maybe even having their own show. And the books! All the books they could write. For them, this was the beginning of a journey that would lead them to fame and fortune. But all Sarah wanted was for Emily to find peace and to learn the truth that haunted them both.

As if he had read her mind, Shane said, "We're not abandoning Emily, Sarah. We can't solve her murder, well yes we can. I mean we can't put her to rest if we don't understand why she is haunting you in the first place. And all that we have will help us understand. We need to educate ourselves."

"I haven't thought of it as a haunting," Sarah said. "That seems so impersonal."

"But that *is* what it is." Todd told her. "Maybe you're in too deep. You need a break. Emotional involvement can be a bad thing when it comes to what we're doing. It's brought a lot of great people to the end of their careers and reputations."

It still didn't feel right and Sarah didn't like it. But she played along, just to keep them all happy, and allowed Shane to take control. Soon at least two dozen 5x7's were spread across her coffee table. Sarah looked them over. She had to admit that they were all downright fantastic, mind boggling and extraordinary in all of their shades of black and gray and white. Before she knew it, she was absorbed in the photos and what Shane was saying and gradually Emily's fate slipped into the back of her mind. She became quite caught up in the simple mystery of life beyond the grave.

Sarah held up a shot of her room, taken from the camera on the far wall. The window glistened with reflected light. One of the other cameras stood like a squat sentry, its tripod legs spread in a wide stance, staring out into the room with one big, round, watchful eye. The night outside of the window seemed pitch-black and endless. The entire world appeared to have been crammed into her room. Six teens. Three cameras on tripods. A video camera. Her bed and all the rest of it. How in the world had she sat there reading for hours on end and not even realize what was going on?

In the photo she could see translucent spheres. Slightly out of focus but with defining edges, they hovered, symmetrically, over the floor. Sarah sat in the dead center of the angle they created. She could see herself through one shadowy orb. There was, she saw, a ghostly barrier between herself and the others.

"Look here," Shane said laying two photos side by side.

They all moved in closer, looking intently at the photos. Each one revealed two very large rather misshapen orbs near the window.

"See how the light seems to pass through this orb here, but not this one?" Shane said, pointing to the identical orb standing next to the first.

"What are you thinking?" Dennis asked.

"I'm thinking one is Emily and the other is Farrell," Shane answered, sitting back to allow the others to study the photos.

"Let me guess which is which," Todd said.

"They look like they're facing each other," Sarah said. "Imagine a face on each of them. Now, doesn't it look like two people facing each other?"

"It does!" Jamie exclaimed. "Do you think we've reunited them? Could we have done that?"

"Slow down!" Shane said, loudly. "It's too soon to assume that we have or even *can* do anything. We don't even know if they are Emily and Farrell at all. Right now all that we have are two very large, very human-shaped orbs."

"You're kidding, right?" Todd asked, bewildered.

"What's wrong with you, Shane?" Dennis asked, his voice cracking in disbelief. "I'd think that you, of all people, would be jumping all over this. This is what you live for! Isn't it?"

Shane didn't respond. Instead he fidgeted, flipping the edges of the photos. He didn't seem like himself. Instead he appeared to be nervous and unsure. And Shane was never unsure about anything.

Something inside Sarah quivered. She knew he was hiding something. Shane was always composed, always bold and spoke his mind. This sudden change of behavior had her suspicious that he'd experienced something like this before. With a raised eyebrow, she asked, "What is it, Shane?"

"I made a mistake once," he said. "Two years ago, I thought I had concrete evidence and I jumped the gun and ran my mouth off. It was the worst year of my life. The entire town called me names. Parents wouldn't let their kids hang out with me. It was horrible. I don't want to go through that again. Not until we know for sure what we are talking about."

"Spooky Shane," Sarah said.

Shane turned on her with the darkest look she'd ever seen. Hot anger flushed his cheeks and a very pained shadow darkened his eyes. "Who told you that?" he demanded.

"No one here, I promise!" Sarah said, sorry that she had said it. Apparently she had hit a sore spot. "I've heard it whispered around school. Remember, I'm the new kid on the block. I only hear things by accident. No one has ever spoken about you to me."

The color started to fade from his cheeks and he sat back down. Still, he seemed troubled.

"You're not jumping the gun here," Sarah told him. "These are not orbs. No way. We've got real stuff. You even said it yourself."

"I had real stuff then, too. Look." Shane withdrew a folder and took out an 8 x 10.

They looked at the photo in disbelief. Bright white snow blanketed trees and an old building. Two very distinct faces came out of nowhere. They shot right out of the building aiming for the camera, their mouths etched in eternal frowns, their eyes narrow and full of rage.

"When was this taken?" Todd asked, turning the photo around.

"About two years ago. That's the old McKinney building," Shane answered.

"Crazy McKinney's?" Jamie asked. "The one he burned to the ground because he swore it was possessed?"

"The one and only," he said.

"This is great. Why did you get so much grief over this?" Sarah asked, remembering that two years ago she was still in Boston dealing with the fact that her father had left them.

"Because this is the blown up shot of the original," Shane said, pulling out another photo from the folder and placing it next to its larger sibling. "I made the enlargement last night."

The original showed the snow encrusted trees, the dark creepy building, as well as two medium sized orbs but nothing out of the ordinary. The orbs could have been snowflakes for anyone's guess.

"I ran around swearing that those orbs were ghosts or even demons. I was laughed at, ridiculed, even warned to keep my mouth shut or my parents would get in trouble. Anyway, I took this to a professional photographer and asked for his opinion. He wrote them off as snowflakes and that was it. I didn't believe him and he knew I didn't. But he wasn't going to admit anything."

"What photographer?" Jamie asked. "It wasn't Landers was it?"

"As a matter of fact, it was. Why?"

"Because he retired a couple of years ago," Jamie said. "That doesn't strike you as coincidence?"

"You think he retired because of my picture?" Shane asked.

"Maybe. Either way, you said you didn't believe him. Why'd you blow these up anyway?"

"When I developed the ones of Sarah's room I remembered McKinney's. I thought I would blow it up, see if the orbs became clearer. This is what I got," he said.

That something inside of her went from quivering to a full body-numbing tremble. Every part of her felt like she was on fire. She didn't want to know, but she *had* to know. Clearing her throat, she asked, "Did you blow *these* up?"

"Yes, I did," Shane said.

With each of those three words, electric shocks ricocheted through her. In that instant, she knew she was not going to like what was about to be revealed.

Chapter 24

The silence that followed was combustible. Everyone waited for Shane to reveal more. He knew something. That was obvious, it showed in the way he fidgeted, in the way he refused to look at any one of them, especially Sarah. She knew that they were all thinking the same thing. Shane had something serious. She waited impatiently, watching as Shane clenched his teeth.

"Hand them over," Dennis said, palm out flat and wanting.

"Why are you holding out?" Todd demanded, speaking at the same time.

Sarah stared him down. Despite the sudden cold that crept along her spine, up her neck and into her skull, she believed they had a right to see whatever it was he had. *She* had the right to know.

"Hand them over," she said severely. Moving with lightning quick grace, she swiped the photos out of his hand.

In the first photo the details of her bedroom were clear and well defined. As always, the shades of black, white and gray were perfect with shadows clinging to the edges of anything solid. She searched for the large, misshapen orbs that she now knew were not orbs but people. But they weren't there, not a single spectral blob, not even a swirl of darkness. There was just her bed, the window, her dresser, the camera and nothing else.

"There's nothing special about this," she said, frowning. "The orbs didn't even show up on the reprint."

Disappointment washed over her. Stubbornly, she studied the photo again, determined to find something. When she did, it was far from what she was hoping to see. It came at her fast, like a bullet, ripping through her mind and shattering all sense of rhyme and reason. In a fit of uncontrollable fear, Sarah threw the pictures at Shane and backed up to the doorway.

"Shane," she cried, "this is a low down, filthy trick!"

Everyone looked over at her, startled. But Shane said nothing, made no attempt to defend himself.

"Hello! What's going on here?" Todd asked.

"Sarah?" Jamie asked. "What's wrong honey?"

"It's not funny, not at all." Sarah addressed Shane directly. "Why'd you do it? Did you think that you'd pull a little bit of BS on me? What have I done to you? Is this your sick sense of humor shining through? *That* would be funny. I didn't think you had a sense of humor!"

"My god, Sarah! Calm down!" Jamie said, putting an arm around her. "Okay, one of you two needs to explain to us dummies over here what in the world is going on."

Sarah shrugged off Jamie's arm and continued to look at Shane as though he had suddenly become her worst enemy.

"I swear to you on my life, this is not a joke," he said, picking up the photos. "All I did was enlarge the original. This is real and it goes beyond the 'whodunit' mystery. I can't explain it. I wish I could. But I swear to you, I didn't tamper with these."

Sarah clenched her fists. One part of her wanted to believe Shane was telling the truth. However, how could it be true? How could something that outrageous be real? Her fear turned to anger, flushing her cheeks.

"What did you do, Shane?" Jamie cried out. "Sarah would not be this upset over nothing."

"I swear I didn't do anything!" Shane said.

"Holy freaking cow!" Dennis said, stealing the pictures from Shane's hands. "Please tell me this is a joke."

"What?" Todd said in an exasperated voice.

"Look real carefully," Dennis said, handing him the photographs. "What is different between these and the original?"

"I still don't - hold on, wait a second. No way! Holy crap, this is great!" Todd exclaimed, dancing up and down.

"I swear to all of you. I didn't do a thing to that photo," Shane said quietly.

"Come on, guys," Jamie said, encircling Sarah with both arms "tell me what's going on."

"I'm not in the picture," Sarah said, her voice wavering.

"Let me see those!" Jamie demanded.

Todd handed them to Jamie as Sarah wiggled out of Jamie's embrace. She couldn't stand to look at those pictures again. Not ever!

The original one had shown her sitting on the edge of the bed, diary in hand, reading. In the enlarged reprint the image was exactly the same, except the bed was totally empty. There was not even an indentation on the comforter. The disappearance of the orbs was explainable; they had been dust after all. But how could a living, breathing person just vanish?

Emily and Farrell had disappeared from the photos. And in doing so, they had taken her along, as if she, too, were nothing more than a ghost.

Chapter 25

Sarah paced the living room, stopping occasionally to wipe away a rebellious tear. How was it possible she that disappeared from the photo? Would Shane do something like that? What had she done, by opening up the door to Emily and Farrell? Wait. She didn't open any doors between life and death. Emily found her. Farrell haunted *her*. She had done nothing at all!

"So what do we do now?" Dennis said, interrupting her thoughts.

Sarah stopped pacing and turned to Shane. She wasn't going to do anything further, *that* she knew, but she waited for his reply.

Shane shrugged. "We can try to recreate the scene," he

said. "Have Sarah read and take more photos."

"I will not!" Sarah said abruptly. "I'm not going to just poof," she snapped her fingers, "disappear again."

"Come on Sarah," Shane said. "You're here, aren't you? No one can make you disappear. Think about it. We have to find out why and how this happened."

"Why? So you can fake more photos and get famous? Is that it, Shane? Is this about *your* glory?" She didn't know why she was so angry with him, but she was. She had wanted no part of this in the first place. Maybe it was all a game, after all.

"Sarah," Shane said, "I swear to you as your friend, I have nothing to do with this. It is not about me. It's about you and these ghosts. Can't you understand that?"

She was confused and scared. She didn't know what she understood anymore. It was too much.

"We can do more research," Jamie offered. "You know, find out if anything like this has ever happened before."

"I say we back off," Sarah said, regaining control of her emotions.

"Back off?" Todd asked, incredulous.

"Yes. Back off. Leave it alone. Put Emily and Farrell to rest. No more photos, no more diary, no more digging into the past. No more."

"I don't think-" Shane began, and broke off as a thunderous roar rolled through the house, shaking the windows and with it, a gust of wind so strong that it brought Sarah to her knees. Riding the wind was a stench so bad that it made everyone gag.

"Ugh! That's disgusting!" Jamie cried out. "It's making my

eyes water."

Everyone coughed and groaned, Todd turned horribly pale and Sarah was afraid he was going to pass out.

Coughing, gasping for breath, Sarah managed to get to her feet. But the roaring continued until she was certain that her head would split open.

"No more!" she screamed.

A low, deep growl reverberated down the hallway. The diary flew up from the sofa and spun several times before smashing into the wall near Sarah's head.

A shadow spilled across the floor. Oozing out of the far corner it stretched until coming to the center of the room.

The shadow brushed over Shane's foot, leaving him ghastly white. Sarah could see Shane's breath cloud before him in a vaporous mist.

"No, Farrell," Sarah said, picking up the diary and flinging it back at the shadow. "I will not read anymore. Read it yourself."

As the Specters huddled together, the shadow recoiled with a howl of rage. Jamie held out her hand for Sarah to join them but as she began to move the shadow moved faster.

Lightning quick and surprisingly solid, a hand grabbed Sarah and yanked her to the floor.

"Farrell, knock it off," she said as forcefully as she could, determined not to let him see her fear.

"Read," hissed a disembodied voice.

"Where's a tape recorder when you need one?" Todd said.

"Shut up!" Shane snapped.

"I'll read it," Jamie said, breaking free of the circle.

"NO!" Another gust of wind pushed the diary out of Jamie's reach.

"Why me?" Sarah demanded.

"Emily!" the voice cried out. All the mourning in the world could have been bottled up in that voice. It was heartbreaking to hear.

"I am not Emily," Sarah cried. "Look at me. I am not Emily!" She felt as if she were barely holding on to her sanity. In a moment or two she was going to crack. She knew it.

Farrell, on the other hand, seemed not to care. The pages of the journal were flipped over, one after another until a photograph fell free of the yellowed pages.

"Oh my god!" Sarah cried softly.

"Hey, she looks just like you!" Dennis said.

It seemed as if Sarah had somehow disappeared from the photo taken in her own bedroom and had materialized in a photograph taken decades ago. She ran a finger over the image. The girl had her nose, her mouth, and her dark hair hung in loose curls just like Sarah's. Behind her was a large brick house facing a rose garden. The Sheriff's house.

"Emily," Sarah whispered.

"Emily," Farrell pleaded.

Suddenly, Sarah was overwhelmed by sorrow. He wanted her to read Emily's diary so he could learn the truth. But she was too drained, too empty inside.

"I can't," she said. "I simply can't."

Again, the stormless thunder ripped through the house. The doors, already shut, opened on their own only to be slammed shut again and the temperature dropped. Tables slid inches out of place, and pictures lost their grips on the wall. The lamps on the end tables danced in place until it seemed the entire house was about to come tumbling down on top of them. Farrell had become the big bad wolf and they were the helpless pigs hiding in the house made of straw.

"I'll read it!" Sarah cried out. "Just not today."

The shadow that was Farrell retreated, spilling backwards into the corner he'd come out of.

Everyone jumped forward and grabbed Sarah, pulling her into one enormous group hug.

"Are you okay?" they asked.

"I think so," Sarah said wearily, feeling as though she had just survived a tornado.

"She looks just like you," Shane said, looking down at the picture in her hand.

Sarah kept her eyes on Emily's image. Her entire body felt stiff. What if they couldn't solve Emily's murder? Would she end up meeting the same fate?

Chapter 26

Whatever intentions the Specters had of pushing the question of Emily's murder aside went right out the window after Farrell's visit. He had, after all, made it ominously clear that her story was far more important that the fact that they were ghosts.

Sarah was true to her word. Drained of every bit of energy, she fell into a sound sleep less than an hour after Farrell's temper tantrum, after making everyone leave and stashing the diary back into its cubbyhole, making sure the bed's leg stood on top of it.

By the time she woke up, early night was pouring into her room along with a warm humid breeze that shuffled the drapes along the floor. Going to stand by the window, she stared out at the violet hued yard and the ominous woods beyond, darker now because time had thickened the growth of trees.

And then, as she watched, mesmerized, two ghostly figures pushed through the trees. Somehow Sarah knew one of them was Emily running to the cemetery. The other ran swiftly, disappearing fully into the thickness of the woods. She wondered if it was Farrell, running after Emily until he stopped by that massive oak tree.

Was it possible that the Sheriff could take down a bear of a man like Farrell, a man whose size combined with a volatile temper? Was it conceivable that someone could have bested him?

"He caught you off guard, didn't he?" she whispered.

The drapes swung wide, revealing the moon that had broken free of clinging clouds and was now shining bright upon the trees, creating a silver highway from her house to the path. The path seemed to call out to her, enticing her to follow.

She'd be stark raving mad to go out there, she thought at first, but then, drawn by a force she didn't understand, she slid on a pair of sweatpants and old sneakers.

Tiptoeing past her mother's bedroom, she made her way to the kitchen and found the flashlight next to the back door. As carefully as she could, she rummaged through odds and ends in the drawer near the sink until she found a small canister of pepper spray. She had no idea if it would work against angry spirits, but she shook the can to make sure it was still full.

Grimacing as the door creaked open, she slid out into the night, the memory of her last venture through the trees flashed through her mind. Clearly, she remembered each vicious blow that had finally defeated Farrell. The image of the devastated, hopeless look upon his face, as he had looked up at her, churned her stomach. This time, however, she hoped to learn something more. She couldn't put words to what it was she thought she might find out. All she knew was that there was more to Farrell's story and that it was just as important to learn, as was Emily's.

The aged picture of Emily surfaced behind her eyes. She stopped and the night closed in around her, like a predator, while the crickets and owls chorused in the muggy darkness.

Common sense told her that the only explanation for the similarity between her and Emily was that they were somehow related. And that thought paralyzed her. With only a few feet separating her from the woods, she stood, breathing hard. Related. It made sense. That was why Emily had reached out to her in the first place. That was why Farrell felt so passionately about her, even his anger. It also explained the weird pull Sarah felt in her heart. And her determination to solve Emily's murder.

There were other things, too. Hadn't Mr. Brewler looked at her oddly on their first visit? It was almost as if he had recognized her. But that wasn't possible. Still, she had seen something cross his face. How had she forgotten that? And then there had been the second visit, when he had stared her down. She could still remember how is his eyes drilled into her. Perhaps the Sheriff had had pictures of Emily, and even though Mr. Brewler hadn't been born yet, they still could have been kept and passed along from one generation to the next. Maybe, even after he had murdered her, he had kept the photos as a memento. It was a twisted thought, but people had been known to do worse.

A hazy white form fluttered through the trees above the path. An owl cried 'who?'. Walking briskly, Sarah found the path and made her way down it. She was already deep into the trees before she realized she hadn't even bothered to turn on the flashlight. Somehow she knew how to navigate the dangerously overgrown path practically blind, as though she had walked it many times before.

When she reached the cemetery, she came to a halt. In the night the grave markers looked like shapeless black ghouls, waiting to pounce upon her as soon as she stepped foot onto their precious grass. However, one caught her attention and drew her toward it as though she were magnetized.

The body of the monument glistened milky white. Moonlight caught on the tiny diamond like chips in the marble and ignited a fairy glow that flickered all along its tall, sharply cut sides.

Sarah made her way to the marble stone. Even in the summer's heat its surface was cool to the touch as she pressed herself against it, loving the feel of the cool smoothness against her cheek.

Emily had died here.

That thought broke the odd peace she was feeling. On the other side of the cemetery there was a well-traveled road leading into the neighboring town several miles south. Once upon a time that road had lead to a certain house.

"You were trying to get to the Sheriff's house, weren't you?" Sarah asked the shadows.

What puzzled her was why Emily would do that. If the Sheriff had been chasing her down, after having killed Farrell, why in the world would she run right for his house? The obvious answer was that it was the fastest route into town. Had she gone the other way, down the long road, she could never have escaped him. Perhaps she thought she could wake up his household and beg them to let her in and help her. That had to have been a better option than the infinite woods. There was help and hope on the other side of the cemetery. But nobody had been able to help her because she had never made it past the monument.

Sarah had no idea how long she stood there, staring around the moonlit burial ground. Before she knew it the moon had swung low across the sky and she became aware that she was no longer alone.

Chapter 27

Dressed in the same thin white gown that fell in gentle folds around her slim body, Emily seemed to float through the wet grass, her hair, loose on her shoulders, glistened in the starlight. She was an angel moving among the long forgotten, a silent song on her lips.

Inching her way around the statue in order to see better, Sarah watched, breathless, as Emily trailed her fingers along the headstones, spinning about at times, so carefree and beautiful.

Suddenly, she stopped, as though startled. Her back stiffened, shoulders squared, her hands clenched into fists.

Emily's voice was misty, fading in and out, so that Sarah

had to move closer to hear what she was saying. She kept low to the ground and listened.

"What are you doing here?" She heard Emily say.

Oh if only she could have heard the answer! But she could not.

"Of course Farrell knows where I am," Emily said, sounding somehow disconcerted. "What about you? Does your father know you're out this late?"

She was lying. Sarah knew that Farrell had never known about the cemetery. And whose father was she referring to? A cold realization hit Sarah like a brick. She had no idea where it had come from or where it would lead. But the thought packed an awful punch. The Sheriff's son, Little Edmond.

Sarah remembered the one passage in the diary about the time Little Edmond had brought Emily flowers.

"I was just about to go back to the house," she heard Emily say. "Thank you for the flowers."

Sarah watched as Emily turned to leave, but her body jerked back forcefully, as if a strong hand had grabbed her shoulder.

"You're hurting me," Emily cried. "Let me go!"

Suddenly, she threw herself backward, straight toward Sarah. No! Not toward her. *Through* her! Emily slammed into the monument. It seemed as if someone was - yes! Someone was pinning her against the stone. Someone Sarah could not see. Emily cried something about telling someone and then Sarah heard a slap and saw a welt form beneath her eye, saw her fall, saw that invisible someone yank her back up by her hair. Sarah could only imagine what was happening, as she spied Emily struggling. Finally, Emily found the strength to push herself away and strike out at him before she turned and ran, only to be caught up again and battered. Sarah couldn't stand it any more.

"Stop it! Stop it!" Sarah shouted.

Flinging her arms left and right, she ran forward, battling the night like a mad woman. Emily slumped against the marble stone, half standing half kneeling. She looked towards Sarah. And this time, Sarah knew she was looking at her, with recognition and purpose.

"I'm so sorry this happened to you," Sarah said, tears streaming down her face.

Emily tried to say something, but the night stole her voice.

"I can't hear you," Sarah said.

"Read," Emily said in a barely audible whisper. Then she faded into nothingness.

Chapter 28

"I'm reading," Sarah said when Jamie opened her eyes and asked what she was doing.

"Well, I can see that," Jamie said, yawning. "But I mean why? It's the middle of the night."

"Because Emily told me to," Sarah snapped. "Now hush up and listen! She's telling about what happened when she came home from the cemetery all bruised. Hush and listen, I need to find out what happened."

I told him right away what Little Edmond had done. I have never seen him so angry as when I told him this. About half an hour later, he was back, dragging

Little Edmond after him, with his father following. I was terrified! There I was, surrounded by all three. Right here in the house Farrell and the Sheriff had fought. At first it was just yelling back and forth. Farrell demanding something be done and the Sheriff trying to explain he was just a boy and he'd handle it at home. Farrell did not like this and said that he needed to learn his lesson now. I could barely stand to listen to them! All the while Little Edmond remained silent. Several times he looked my way and I swear the corner of his mouth lifted, as if mocking me. In the end, Sheriff Brewler left with his son. Before leaving, the sherriff gave me a look I can't begin to describe nor understand. All I know is that I believe it's time to forget the Brewlers entirely.

Sarah closed the diary, unable to believe what she had just read. He was only a boy! Younger than Emily was herself. Yet, he had done the vicious beating she'd witnessed herself. Sarah realized she was crying. Jamie handed her a tissue and they both wiped their eyes.

It was all beginning to sound like a soap opera. If it hadn't been for ghosts, dreams, visions and the actual photograph of Emily, Sarah would have discarded the diary as the scribbling of a young woman with a very overactive imagination.

"Are you going to read more?" Jamie asked, grabbing a new tissue.

"Are you serious?"

"Come on, we need to see what else happens," Jamie said.

Sarah opened the diary again, breathing deep, she continued.

> He came back only a few days after the incident. The Sheriff had indeed beaten him, quite severely. I could see yellowish bruises around his eyes and cheeks. He said he had come to apologize. He was so different this time. He was charming and handsome. However, when I thought he was going to leave, he grabbed me and tried to kiss me! He is even more persistent than his father. It scares me. He won't take no for an answer and gets so angry so quickly. I am afraid of him. Terrified really.

"At least she was smart enough to know he was trouble," Sarah said.

"Right. But where did it get her?" Jamie asked.

"Sometimes I wonder if I shouldn't just pack up and go," Sarah read.

> I think Farrell would understand. Yet, each time I am ready to start packing, I think of Farrell and his oddly handsome face, the way his hands sometimes brush my arm or back, so tender. And I can't do it. Then I think of how lonely he is. I was just like him, and he saved me. I can't leave him.

"That's odd," Jamie said.

"What is?"

"All of a sudden she just stops mentioning either one of the Brewlers. Little Edmond beats her then comes back and tries to kiss her, for one. And she's obviously in love with the sheriff, yet doesn't mention either one," Jamie said.

"Maybe she does, hold on."

Sarah flipped through the diary. Five blank pages followed the last one she'd read and one page had something scrawled so illegibly she couldn't make heads or tails out of it. She said as much to Jamie but looked up to see that Jamie had drifted off to sleep. Sarah yawned, stretching, but she wasn't ready to stop reading.

Anna Brewler died today. I do not dare go to her services this morning. I must respect the Sheriff in his time of grief. While he grieves, I daydream about the times we'd walk around the cemetery, laughing and kissing. But now I am afraid of who could be there waiting for me. It isn't a secret anymore, and no longer seems safe. The beauty of it is gone. When I felt Little Edmond's cruel hands, all the wonderful things of that place vanished. Like so many things before, it is just a place to go to in my dreams.

After turning two more blank pages, Sarah read the next passage with a sinking heart. It wasn't like reading a novel anymore. Now she could feel every word Emily wrote. When she read, she could hear Emily's voice, hear her thoughts, and though it seemed impossible, feel what Emily must have felt.

Farrell approached me tonight and although he had been drinking, he was far from drunk. He came to me while I sat in bed, reading. He knelt beside me and took my hands in his and kissed me full on the lips. Then he turned very red and practically ran out of the room.

I remained awake almost until dawn. Whatever am I to do? Isn't this what I've been waiting for? Hasn't his coolness and indifference been the one thing that kept pushing me into the Sheriff's arms?

Oh my troubles only seem to increase! Autumn is ending and already the winter chill is creeping into the air. I feel such an odd sense of urgency. It feels as if time is running out and I must make a decision. I have no idea what decision to make, though. I will have to hurt one of them. Farrell has no one but me, but he's tougher and doesn't need a woman's love to hold him together. The Sheriff has his family but he is in need of love. What am I to do? How do I make a decision and should I even? I still wonder if I should just go away.

A rock hit my window and to my horror, I found Little Edmond outside. I haven't seen him since the day he apologized.

I didn't know what to do! What was he doing outside my window in the night? He told me that it was urgent, and that his father was seriously ill and that he is asking for me.

Oh! I will be braving so much, but I have to see him. And I will, first thing in the morning.

Chapter 29

Sarah tried to catch her breath, and imagined Emily doing the same thing when she had written these words.

A bit of paper sticking out from the book's bind caught Sarah's eye. She realized that pages had been ripped out. Had Farrell done it? No, they had been taken out too neatly, care taken not to damage the existing pages. What, she wondered, would Emily have wanted to remove?

Now that Jamie was sound asleep again, Sarah allowed herself to melt into the narration, to slip into the past, and live Emily's life just as she had lived it.

I will write this in as much detail as I can and I swear I will not stop writing

until every last detail has been accounted
for!

I have never been so terrified. Never, in
all of my life, have I known such demonic
cruelty. And all from a boy slightly younger
than I!

As I promised, shortly after Farrell
left, I stole away to the Sheriff's house
and found it quiet. Little Edmond opened
the door and told me that his father was
in the downstairs bedroom, and that he
was still very ill but would not allow
anyone but me come see him.

No one seemed to be about as the
house was completely still. I should
have known something was wrong! How it
happens that I am alive to write this, I do
not know.

When Little Edmond led me to a
bedroom, the bed was empty. Before I
could protest, he had shut and locked the
door.

" I don't understand," I said." Where's
your father?" Fear soured my stomach and
all I wanted was to get out into the fresh
air.

He just stood there, a wicked grin on
his face. I think this is when I began

to shake. I don't think I've ever been so afraid in all my life! The night in the cemetery came back fresh and clear and I swear I could feel the bruises all over.

"Edmond," I said as sternly as I could, "let me out this instant or I swear I will start screaming and I won't stop until someone comes and tears down that door!"

"Go ahead," he said. "Everyone, including the maids and the cook, are at my mother's grave right now, paying their respects. See, you don't know everything about my stupid father. He loves my mother, even though you tried to seduce him!"

"What are you talking about? Let me go home." When he said I had seduced his father I grew hot with anger! How dare he? He didn't know anything about his father and I.

"You should be with me," he told me, his face softening just a little. "I can love you far better than he can. He's old and decrepit. I am fresh and young, like a young woman should want."

I couldn't comprehend all the nonsense about me being with him! I just wanted out of that room. I had turned my back to him, trying again, to open the door.

That's when he practically screamed at me.

"Look at me!"

Before I knew it he was grabbing me, forcing me to turn around and look at him. I adverted my eyes, staring down at my feet. I couldn't think. I could barely breathe, I was so scared!

"Look at me, dammit!" He stroked my hair, snatching a handful and letting it run between his fingers. I didn't like the feeling of it, not at all.

"You see, my love," he whispered in my ear, "I am the man for you. Not my father and never that drunkard you live with."

Then he went on to tell me about how strong of a man he was, how he was born for me and a whole speech that still makes no sense to me at all.

Then he began tugging on my hair. Again, the night in the cemetery came back fresh and hot! I was shaking so bad and this seemed to please him, as he tugged harder.

"Let me go home," I said as boldly as I could. "I do not want you nor need you."

"No?" he said, his lips pressed against my ear. "Oh I think you do." He tried to kiss me, but I turned my head. His teeth caught in my hair. He growled like some animal.

"Admit it," he said and then he bit me!

I yanked away from him so fast strands of my hair remained entwined between his fingers. I banged on the door as hard as I could, I didn't care if I broke any bones. I hammered and screamed for help!

"It's just you and me, my love," he said, pressing me against the door. These words haunt me even now. I can't get them out of my head.

"Edmond Brewler, Jr." I yelled. "Let me out of here right now!" I fisted my hands. I swore I'd hit him! But he just laughed.

"And I told you," he practically hissed. "Not until I decide it. And never," with these words he yanked my head back, banging it against the door. "Never call me junior again! I am nothing of my father. Do you understand me?"

It amazes me how I can remember all of this in such vivid detail. But my mind won't let it go. The whole scene keeps replaying over and over until I am nauseous. But I feel that I must write it all down.

My hands tremble to recount these

events.

He is a monster! He slapped me hard across the face, knocking me to the floor. Then, like bullets, his fists battered my head, back and arms. He hit me so fast and so hard it felt like ten hands pounding me, not two. I remember crying and trying to hide my face in my arms. Yanking me by my hair, he pulled me to my feet and unleashed a furious rage. He beat my breasts, my stomach, and my thighs.

I look like a plum! I am blue, purple, red, yellow and a disgusting shade of green and black from my thighs to my shoulders. Even my breasts are bruised and scraped raw in places from his rough hands.

I am not sure how long it took, but finally exhausted, he flung himself upon the bed, leaving me crumpled on the floor. He was so arrogant that he paid me no mind. Not the fact that I was bleeding nor that I would do my best to escape.

I admit that for several moments all I could do was stare at him, hatred filling me like mud. Then I remembered the key. It was in his pants. I tiptoed over to him and carefully pulled the key free. I had it in the lock and had just started to turn it when suddenly he was behind me.

172 | Joann Reneé Muszynski

"Where do you think you're going?" he asked.

"Home," I said. "I hate you."

Then I asked him if his father treated his mother this way. I could feel his breath on my neck and I knew that I had angered him in a very bad way. I could already sense his hands preparing for another beating.

"Let me go home," I whispered.

"Promise me that you will come back to me," he said. "Whenever I want you to. Not my stupid father, Emily. Promise me that and I will let you go."

I did the only thing I could think of, I promised.

Farrell was at the back door waiting for me. How he knew I'd be coming right then I have no idea. I threw myself into his arms and confessed everything. I begged him to let me stay and protect me from that horrible, evil monster.

Chapter 30

How she managed an entire week of keeping her sanity, Sarah had no idea. The days sped by in a blur. She could not remember what she ate, if she ate, or anything else that she did. All she could remember was Emily's face, bruised and torn, and the heartache that carried her to her grave.

When Saturday came, she agreed to meet with the Specters, although she didn't know how she could possibly concentrate on what the others were saying. Still, she drove with Jamie across town to a lovely park where they sat on the shore of the lake and watched the shimmering ripples.

They had been talking for a while, but Sarah hardly knew what was being said. Her mind kept wandering off down a dark narrow path where the smell of pine was strong. Every now and then she'd come back and hear bits and pieces of conversation; "and I know that … I believe it's time..." Yet she could not put a complete sentence together. However, something must have caught her attention because she apparently made a response that Jamie, at least, found inappropriate.

"Look at you, Sarah!" she said angrily. "I don't think you should argue with anyone!"

What had she said? What was Jamie talking about?

"Listen," Shane was saying, "we're all fascinated by this. We are all intrigued with Emily's story, but -"

Instantly, Sarah came to life.

"An intrigue?" she said. "Is that all it is to you guys? Just like some old Nancy Drew book? Oh, please! We are in this so deep we can't even walk straight."

"You're the only one who is in this that deep," Todd said.

"We're worried about you," Kate told her, her pale face a little moon in the bright afternoon sun.

Sarah looked at her long and hard. Was Kate, she wondered, really one of them? She had never seemed completely involved, always there but with a bit of disconnect about her.

"What makes you think you have any reason to be worried?" Sarah said.

"Have you looked in a mirror recently?" Todd asked her. "You're all shallow and pale. You look like you've lost weight and you have circles under your eyes. Of course, you could be going for that Gothic look, but I don't think those black smudges are makeup."

"The point is that we," Shane said. "Particularly you, Sarah, have allowed ourselves to become pre-occupied with Emily. It's time to back off. We need to live normal teen-age lives. School starts in a couple of weeks. I say we wait and get the new school year started then slowly work our way back into this."

Everyone agreed, except Sarah, who sat there, staring off into space again. Could it really be true that summer was over? But it seemed as though it had just begun. Maybe she *was* in too deep.

And then she told herself that no, she wasn't. Emily needed her.

"We can't let go now, guys," Sarah said, getting to her feet and staring down at their upturned faces. "She needs us. She's begging for our help. Even if she is targeting me, she needs all of us. *I* need all of us. Emily's holding on because she believes that we can pull through for her. Isn't it true that some ghosts only appear for a reason, Shane?"

"What do you think she wants us to do?" he asked.

"Get the truth out. Everyone who knew her believes Farrell killed her and then just disappeared. The Sheriff went to his grave with a very dark secret. His grandson believes that Farrell killed Emily. It's all lies. Emily wants the truth to be known. And Farrell needs to know she didn't betray him."

"Maybe you're right," Shane said thoughtfully.

Groaning, Dennis hung his head between his knees while Todd threw himself backward and stared up into the cloudless blue sky.

"I just want to be a kid again!" Todd muttered.

"Look, none of you are bound to this," Shane said. "You

can walk away at any time you want to. All I meant was that I'm here for Sarah."

"And you know I am always here for you, too," Jamie said, reaching for Sarah's hand. "I'm worried about you and all. But if you need me, I'm here."

"Me, too," Kate said.

"Oh great, make us out to be the bad guys," Dennis complained. "Yeah, yeah, whatever. I'm a Specter, and that means I am a part of the team, all the time. Fine, I'm in."

They all turned to look at Todd.

"What? Of course I'm in. You need me more than anyone else, anyway," he said, smiling his crooked smile.

In that moment, Sarah could feel the bond of friendship between them. She basked in it, as she had never felt it before.

Chapter 31

"I need to show you guys something in the cemetery," Sarah said, pulling Jamie to her feet. "Come on."

Half an hour later, they were parked on the dirt road that forked off the main highway. Sarah led them to a massive, age-old oak tree at the far southern corner. It towered above them, shading them from the hot sun with its enormous leafy head.

"This was where Emily and the Sheriff met," Sarah said. And then she went on to tell them about Little Edmond and what Emily wrote about her trip to his house that one awful day.

She tried to recite the diary as best she could, surprising herself at just how much she actually remembered. She found the words easy to conjure up, the emotion to put behind them almost natural.

Suddenly, she had an idea.

"What if we try to conjure them up again," she said. "But in a different way. We could try to get Emily and Farrell in the same room, like before. Only this time try to *really* get them together. And get it all on tape."

"First you're terrified beyond belief, now you want to conduct séances?" Todd asked, clearly amused.

"Séance is such a crappy word. That's not what we will be doing. I'm saying we should just repeat what we did last time. Only this time, when they appear, we acknowledge their presence," she told him.

"Are you sure you don't want to just let them go back to their graves?" Kate asked.

"They can't," Sarah answered. "Not until we tell them the truth."

"Maybe we should just let them go," Jamie said softly.

The enemy, doubt, raised its battle sword again. Sarah's temper grew hot. Jamie's betrayal stung her more deeply than she could have imagined.

"I thought you guys said you were with me," she said. "You know what? Fine, do whatever. I don't need you after all."

Shane jumped to his feet and grabbed her by the arm as she walked past him.

"Stop it," he said. "We're just thinking about you and that you need some rest."

"You're thinking about me and what I need." Sarah heard her voice start to rise. "What about Emily and what she needs?"

She hated the sudden onslaught of emotion that seemed to erupt so easily nowadays.

"Emily is dead," Todd said firmly.

When Shane's grip on her forearm tightened, she thought of Emily and how Little Edmond's hand had gripped her that horrible day, and Shane, sensing that something was wrong, let go of her at once.

"We need to reveal the truth," she said.

"How are we going to do that?" Dennis asked. "We don't know where Farrell is buried. We can't sit over his grave and say, 'Look bud, this is what really happened.'"

"Don't make fun of me," Sarah said.

"I'm not," Dennis said. "I'm just speaking the obvious. God, calm down."

"Emily's family," Sarah said in a low voice.

"You don't know that," Kate said. "Just because the two of you look alike - well, that doesn't prove a thing."

Sarah could see them judging her, detaching themselves from her emotionally. All because she knew things they didn't. All because she had a stronger tie to what they've sworn to believe in. That wasn't her fault.

"It's not just that we have the same color hair and the same build," Sarah insisted. "I mean did you look at her? We are almost identical!"

No one said a word.

"Fine," she said. "Go back to your boring lives of pretending to believe in ghosts. I don't need you."

"That wasn't fair," Shane called after her.

Chapter 32

As she pushed through the trees, the bright light blinded her. Covering her eyes with a hand, she slowed down to a walk, glad to be in her own yard and out of the oppressive darkness of the woods. She was half way across the lawn when she saw them waiting for her.

"I thought I was on my own," she called out to them.

"Well, you know, Emily's not your only family," Jamie said, hugging her.

"We decided," Shane said, "that maybe you're on to something, after all."

Sarah turned to face the woods.

"Pretty soon, I will have the whole story for you, Farrell," she promised.

Something deeper black than the shadows moved through the trees, just barely touching the sunlight filling the yard, quick and silent.

"Uh, did any of you see that?" Dennis asked.

"I guess Farrell heard you," Todd said. "You better deliver on your promise, Sarah. He's watching you."

Sarah shivered. Though she knew he hadn't killed Emily, she still didn't care much for Farrell. His spirit harbored anger and rage. Whatever kindness, love and compassion he had in life had been left behind when he crossed over.

"Mr. Brewler," Sarah said suddenly.

"What about him?" Shane asked.

"Remember how he asked me to tell him the story when we got it all figured out?" she asked. "Well, he's the way to reveal the truth. If I'm a descendant of Emily's family and Mr. Brewler is a direct descendant of the Sheriff and Little Edmond, then if I tell him the truth, wouldn't that put closure to it? Emily's side to the Sheriff's side?"

"Except for Farrell," Todd said.

"Three men loved Emily," Sarah said. "A father and his son were both insanely in love with her. One of them killed her."

"One of them? I thought you knew who did," Dennis said.

"As with all great mysteries, there's always that last twist to throw you off," Sarah said. "We've been thrown off."

"First Farrell was supposed to have killed Emily. Then it was the Sheriff. Now maybe it's his son?" Dennis made a face. "Did you ever think that possibly it wasn't any of them? Maybe

Emily killed Farrell and then killed herself."

"That's not even funny," Jamie said.

"No, but it is a possibility," Dennis said.

"Not really," Sarah said.

Dennis gave Sarah an exasperated look.

"Whatever," he said. "Let's just solve this case and move on. I'm getting exhausted."

"You can quit at any time, Dennis," Sarah said, thinking to herself, *here we go again*.

"I could, but I won't," he said. "We've decided that you could be related to Emily and it could be possible she's communicating with you for a very specific reason. I don't want to miss out on this opportunity."

"Then stop complaining!" she shot back at him.

"Can I complain that I'm starving?" he asked.

"No," Sarah said as she unlocked the back door and let them into the kitchen.

As they ate cold chicken and chips, they sat around the kitchen table and debated what the next step should be.

"I guess we should figure out how far down the family tree Emily is from Sarah," Kate suggested. "At least the research will take us away from the violence for a while." She was a good study in genealogy and the idea of doing some good digging seemed to excite her.

"That's a good idea," Shane said. "You still have that genealogy software you bought for your project last year?"

"Sure do," Kate said.

"Then you're hired. You're the best one to do it," Shane said.

"I would really appreciate it, Kate," Sarah said.

"You know I didn't like you much when we first met, right?" Kate said.

Sarah stared at her, not sure what to say.

"Man, that was rude!" Todd said.

"I'm not finished. I said 'at first,' and I still can't figure you out, but I've decided you're not all that bad. I'll do it."

They waited until Wednesday to get together and discuss what Kate had found. Sarah had given her all the names she knew on both her mother's and her father's side. It wasn't a very long list, since neither side had believed in large families. The largest family had been that of her paternal grandmother who had three children.

Sarah was a riot of nerves, tremendously excited about the possibilities. Maybe Emily was a great aunt. The fact that she would find out that they really did share history and a bloodline thrilled her. It brought her even closer to Emily. She couldn't get Emily out of her head, or ignore Emily's private thoughts. Monday night she had sat up until three o'clock in the morning listening to Emily tell her about her hopes and dreams, all the things she'd never written in the diary.

Now she sat in Kate's living room with a nest of butterflies in her stomach. On the long, blonde-wood coffee table, a series of papers had been laid out in a line, on each one was an outline of a tree. Each branch boasted one surname and the leaves on the branch listed each child born.

It was such a jumble that Sarah had no clue as to what it represented. But for the second time, she saw Kate's magic shine. Clearly she was proud of her work as her face was bright, even more beautiful, if that was possible. Just like when she had shown them the drawing of Emily looking out the window.

Making a paper pyramid, she pointed to the first sheet on which the names Edwards, Stanley and Foxworth appeared. Sarah did not recognize any of them.

It wasn't until they had worked their way down to the middle paper in the last row that Kate grew excited as she pushed the other papers aside

The very first branch was named Thomasford with three leaves of Charles Anthony, Margit Lynn and Dorothy Anne. Bells started to ring inside Sarah's head, she just couldn't put her finger on what it was.

"This is your father's tree," Kate told her.

Chapter 33

Sarah didn't know much about her father's side of the family because he never talked about them and didn't have many photos. She remembered meeting her grandmother a couple of times when she was little, and that her name was Bella Crossfield.

Sure enough, on the Crossfield branch there were three leaves: Adam Walter, Maria Sue and Joseph Daniel, Sarah's father being the youngest of the three. She had never met her aunt or her uncle before. And had never thought to ask why.

Looking up a branch from her grandmother's tree, Sarah saw that her great grandmother had married a Scott Crawford in 1950 and that he had had a brother, Harry. Moving one more branch up the tree, she saw that Dorothy's father had one brother, Thomas Joseph Edding, who married in 1912 and had two daughters.

And there, clearly printed, was the name they had all come to know, Emily Sarah Edding born May 2nd 1913.

Going onto the Internet, Kate pulled up a family charting graph so that they could place the relationship exactly. After close to twenty minutes of working back and forth over the math, they came to a conclusion. Emily and Sarah were first cousins three times removed.

"Man, if that's not confusing," Todd said.

"My cousin," Sarah said softly. There it was in black and white. She and Emily were related without a doubt.

"This is a rare case," Shane said. "There are hundreds of reports of deceased family members lingering in the halls or basements of old homes. But there is less than a handful of ghost relatives that speak up and ask for help. Well, at least you know for sure why Emily chose you over any of us, Sarah."

"Yeah, you're not so special after all," Dennis told her, grinning.

Sarah realized that although it was a little bit of a relief that she wasn't special, as Dennis said, it was a bit disappointing, too. In a mix of emotions, she found that she wanted every possibility to be true. Or perhaps all of them frightened her. She was, to say the least, confused about just how she felt.

Ever since Farrell had shown them the photograph, she'd known without a doubt that she and Emily were related. Yet doubt had kept rearing its ugly head and she had feared that maybe, just maybe, her erratic obsession with this was going to be for naught, that Emily would turn out to be nothing but the ghost of a girl who bore a vague resemblance of her.

But now she knew for certain that she was in this until she could figure out how to put Emily to rest. She only had speculations as to who had killed Farrell and Emily. It could have been one of two people, and one was only a boy, even though she knew that he had a dark side.

"Let's go to the cemetery and take some shots," Shane said.

"That's a good idea," Sarah said, "I want you guys to get some footage around that big tree. Emily and the Sheriff spent a lot of time there. Maybe she'll come by and give us some more information or something."

"One car or all?" Dennis asked.

"Kate's got the van. It's easier that way," Shane said.

Once again they piled into the van with camera bags in tow. As they pulled away from Kate's house, Shane handed Sarah a small leather bag with a fat nylon shoulder strap.

"Here," he said. "This if for you. Consider it a gift."

Sarah pulled out the small, auto focus, auto flash Canon and admired it.

"You might as well learn how to use it," Shane said, wickedness gleaming in his eyes.

"So does that mean I'm an official member of the Specters?" Sarah asked. She was very happy in that moment. She couldn't explain it. But she felt it.

"Of course," Shane said.

Todd gave her one of his wide, gleaming smiles. "You're a valuable asset now," he told her. "You know how to talk to ghosts." Before she knew it, he had taken a single shot of her.

"Here we are," Kate called out over her shoulder as she pulled off the paved road and maneuvered the van over the uneven road, pulling up parallel to the rusted fence.

The day was hot and humid.

"Come on, let's go swimming," Todd said, heading back to the van.

"Get over here," Jamie said.

They hurried for the shade of the tree. Sarah wasn't sure where to start snapping pictures. While the others went right into motion, she walked slowly, searching for anything that might inspire her.

After circling the tree four times, tripping over Dennis as he lay on the ground shooting up into the leaves and nearly knocking Kate to the ground, she decided to just take a few shots. Without relying on any particular technique, she fired away: click, click, click. As she listened to the camera's tiny, mechanical voice she heard it say, 'There's nothing here.'

Since Jamie had the largest dark room, they drove to her house. Sarah and Jamie took their sweet time developing their film while the others finished and went out to the game room to watch TV.

After a while they collected the photos. Shane scowled, Sarah sighed loudly and Dennis offered a few choice words of his own.

"Someone took a very cute shot of a rabbit," Jamie said, holding up the photo. "It's a great shot."

"What now?" Todd asked.

"We'll have to depend on the diary, I guess," Shane said.

"I've already read the rest of it," Sarah said. "Emily didn't write anything after the incidence with Little Edmond at his house. The last page I read was about Emily's decision. She told the Sheriff she wouldn't see him anymore. She told him what Edmond had done and that she could never live in the same house with him. The Sheriff protested, of course, but Emily wouldn't listen to him. The very last entry described her confession to Farrell."

"And that's it?" Dennis asked.

"There was a place not too far from the end where it looked like several pages may have been torn out," Sarah said.

"Well, that's not going to help us," Todd grumbled. "Now what are we supposed to use for gathering info on who killed her? We can't solve the mystery if she doesn't tell us who did it."

"You didn't like the idea of a séance," Shane said, his eyes on Sarah. "How about hypnotism? You've had enough contact with Emily and Farrell," he went on, with his customary wicked grin. "They used your energy to materialize before. Remember the photo where you're missing? What if, and keep an open mind here, we video you while under hypnosis. Maybe you could connect with Emily and she'll lead you into the past. It's not all that different than the visions you've already had."

"Who's going to hypnotize her?" Jamie asked.

"I will," Shane said.

Hypnotism, she thought. Could Shane really pull if off? Or, worse yet, if he did, couldn't it be dangerous?

Chapter 34

Since they found the diary in the bedroom and Emily had slept in the same room, it only made sense for them to try the hypnosis there.

They set up just as they had the time Sarah read from the diary, the video camera standing at the foot of the bed. Sarah lay on her back, holding Emily's photograph pressed to her chest. She was more than nervous. She was terrified. What if Shane didn't know what he was doing? What if she got stuck in the past? Who would come get her?

"Try to stay calm," Shane reassured her, rubbing her arm. "I know what I'm doing. You have to trust me."

His touch was warm and oddly soothing. Sarah closed her

eyes and inhaled then exhaled as deeply as she could.

Dennis and Todd manned two of the Nikons while Kate sat beside the video, sketchpad on her knees, charcoal pencil in hand. Jamie sat to Sarah's right. She was there for support, her hand resting lightly on Sarah's shoulder.

"I'm here," she said. "If anything looks like it's wrong, I will make sure to wake you up. You're going to be okay."

Shane began his instructions.

"Remember, breathe deep and slow. Control every breath. Pull your weight down, through your spine and into the mattress. Forget about me and the cameras. Forget everything. Empty your mind. Okay? Ready? Here we go."

Inhaling as he had told her to, she pulled into herself as deeply as she could, emptying her mind and relaxing every muscle in her body. And then, when her mind was perfectly blank, she filled it with Emily's image.

Suddenly sleep drew itself over her like a blanket. Further and further down she slid and she forgot everything, photography, and ghosts, until she couldn't even hear Shane's voice.

Air filled her lungs. It filled her entire body. It lifted her up and gingerly snaked itself around her ankles. It climbed up her legs, swirled about her hips, and stretched up in tendrils to cling to her breasts.

It was then that she saw the grayness and the mist.

A breeze drifted over her, warm and salty, as though it had come from the sea, blowing apart the colorless mist that clung to her. Reaching down, Sarah tried to grasp it. But it flew through her window and floated away in ribbon like wisps.

"Emily?" she called.

"Follow me," a voice replied. It was a woman's voice, soft and musical and familiar.

She tried to move, but her legs were like lead.

"Move with your mind," the voice told her.

The breeze had become a blissful breath upon her skin. She knew that she could become part of it. She felt herself drift down a path overgrown with gnarled roots that could not touch her, past branches that tried to reach out for her and failed.

Then she was standing on the grassy lawn, looking at the back of her house. A full moon hung low in the sky and inside there was lamplight. Sarah tiptoed across the night-covered lawn and crept up to the kitchen window.

Emily was moving around the kitchen, preparing a meal. Pots steamed on an old fashioned wood burning stove. A vase of wild flowers and pinecones stood in the center of a simple square table.

Emily was whirling around, the pale blue apron she wore lifting and falling as she spun on her toes like a ballerina. She hummed a song as she hurried between the table and the stove and it was clear that she was putting together a special dinner.

The front door creaked open then shut with a hard, solid thud and a shadow moved along the wall. Emily stopped dancing and turned to the entryway. Her hands fluttered like fragile white birds. Her eyes shone big and bright. The softest of pinks spread naturally across her cheeks. She was radiant.

When Farrell arrived, tall and formidable, he stared at Emily, flushed and shy, he was a handsome man whose eyes sparkled with their own strange light. Bringing his hands from behind his back, he held out a bunch of plump, velvety roses, cradled in a nest of white baby's breath.

"They're beautiful!" Emily breathed, hiding her face, which was now aflame. Going to the table, she replaced the wild flowers with the roses he had brought her.

When he called her name, Emily turned and let him take her in his arms. Then they shared the most romantic kiss Sarah had ever seen. And then suddenly a bitter cold engulfed her, sucking away her breath and raking icy fingers down her spine, replacing her blood with ice and worming its way into her lungs, suffocating her.

She stumbled backwards. What did this mean? Was Farrell suffocating Emily and, as a consequence, her as well? But no! As the chill lifted, she could see Farrell handing Emily a little box with gold ribbon. Somehow, she knew that in that moment, Emily had never been this happy before, and never would be again.

Suddenly, something caught her eye. Looking away from the window, she saw *him*.

Chapter 35

Little Edmond crouched low. Dressed in black, he blended perfectly with the night. He watched, nothing more than a shadow, as Emily and Farrell sat down and ate their dinner.

She had never before felt such cold hatred. His hatred for Farrell turned a balmy summer night into an arctic hell.

She could see in the darkness how strong he was, even for a boy. His entire body writhed with tense muscle. His fists clenched and unclenched repeatedly.

Then he moved. With stealth and ease, he glided into the darkness and slipped into the garden, simply melting away until he reappeared at the edge of the garden where he grabbed a young sapling and snapped it in half.

Once she knew that Little Edmond had gone, Sarah ran back to the window. Pressing her face against the glass, she saw Emily and Farrell sitting at the table, drinking wine and laughing, oblivious to the evil outside. Oh how blissful they were. Farrell's face was completely transformed. The mask of tension and anger had fallen away. And Emily, all the love in the world shone bright in her eyes.

Everything began to disappear in a surge of gray mist. Sarah fought against it desperately. She wasn't ready to go! She had to warn Emily. She had to make sure that Little Edmond did not get a chance to do whatever it was he had in mind.

But it was useless. The mist claimed her and pushed her back into the woods. With tears streaming down her cheeks, she turned away and bolted down the path. With each step, her body grew heavier and heavier. Then everything started spinning out of control and with a sickening plummet, she fell downward until she landed on her bed.

When she opened her eyes the light blinded her. Throwing her arms up over her face, she gasped for breath.

"Send me back!" she cried. "Send me back!"

"Sarah!" she heard Jamie say. "Wake up."

"Sarah," other voices cried as she felt hands on her, tugging at her shoulders. She fought them off until, finally exhausted, she found that she could open her eyes and the images of Emily and Farrell were replaced by the faces of her friends. But the awful cold from Little Edmond still clung to her.

"Are you okay?" Shane asked.

"Why did you bring me back?" Sarah demanded.

"You scared us because you were thrashing around,"

Shane said.

"I saw Little Edmond," Sarah said, struggling for breath. "He's scarier than Farrell could ever have been. He was watching them through the kitchen window. Oh, they were so much in love and so happy! Then he left and I was alone again and then the mist came. I didn't want to lose them. I *can't* lose them. Send me back!"

"I don't think that's a good idea," Jamie said. "Look at your arms!"

Dark red fingerprints were imprinted in her skin from her elbows to her wrists.

"Who were you fighting?" Shane asked.

"No one," Sarah insisted. "I was just standing there watching. Then this cold, I mean bitter cold, came over me, it choked me. I had to back away. That's when I saw him and I was so terrified I couldn't move. Honest, that's all that happened."

Had that been all that had happened, though? She tried to recall every detail of what she had seen until she was shaking. Jamie grabbed the extra blanket off the foot of the bed and wrapped it around her. Kate came over and sat on the edge of the bed and held her tight. Even the guys came over and wrapped their arms around her. Suddenly, she was scared. So terribly scared.

Then a thought occurred to her. She didn't like it one bit and prayed that it would never ever happen again.

"I think that we became one person," she said. "Little Edmond and I, but how can that be because he's evil?"

"Let's see if the video can give us any answers," Shane said.

Sarah watched Shane go to the video recorder and rewind

the tape. Hitting play, he lowered his eye to the viewfinder.

"Are you ready for this?" he asked.

Chapter 36

Shane had hooked the camcorder to the television and now, on the screen, Sarah saw herself thrashing about wildly on the bed. And then she was gone.

The tape blipped, and jumped a frame as if power had been momentarily disconnected. In the blink of an eye, the footage was clear. However, Sarah was no longer lying on the bed. A shadow had replaced her, long and lean, its head neatly pushed into the pillows, its hands knitted together on its chest. Emily, cloaked in darkness and barely substantial, lay in Sarah's place, her bosom rising and falling as she breathed exactly the same as Sarah had when Shane had begun to hypnotize her. Perhaps twenty seconds passed then the video blipped again and Sarah once more occupied the bed. Shane leaned over her and tried to wake her up and then it was over.

Shane turned the TV off.

"Send me back," Sarah said again. Something clung to her and it infected her mind. It wasn't the mist, it wasn't even Emily. It was truth. She was so close to knowing the truth.

"No. You've had enough. You need some rest," Shane said.

She knew that no matter what arguments she presented him with, he would not give in and so she simply watched as he busied himself by disconnecting the video equipment and packing it up.

"Listen to me," Sarah said, determined to make one last try. "I have to stop him. Send me back!"

Shane turned on her then and took her by the arms.

"They are dead, Sarah!" he said in a low voice. "You can't prevent it from happening. No more, that's it!"

Backing away from him, Sarah went to the window and, opening it, stared out into the night, her mind was a muddled mess.

"Get some sleep," Shane said. "We'll see you in the morning. Come on guys. You too, Jamie. You know that your mother wants you home tonight."

"You're going to leave me here alone?" Sarah asked.

"Get some sleep," he said, his voice filled with compassion and something she couldn't quite identify. "Take something if you have to. We'll be here first thing in the morning, promise."

Sarah stood there by the window until she heard Kate's van start up and pull off down the drive. She was alone. Oh god, how scary that was! Slipping beneath her covers, she lay on her back for a long time before turning out the light. She still had the photograph of Emily and she held it tight until at last her eyes began to drop. Just when she had drifted off, she felt the all too familiar pull of the past take hold of her. She embraced it, willingly. She hadn't been ready to come back. Now was her chance to return. They were wrong. She *could* stop Little Edmond.

Trees stretched out before her. The cold, windy night whipped their thick leafy heads to and fro, knocking a rainfall of leaves to the ground.

Standing directly in front of her, his eyes glittering in the moonlight, was Little Edmond.

For a long moment, Sarah wasn't sure if she was Emily or not. But when he addressed her, she knew how she appeared to him.

"Where's your lover, Emily?" he sneered.

"He's inside," she told him trying to temper her terror with words.

"Liar," he said.

"What do you want?" she asked. She was trembling, but determined not to let it show, she clenched her hands into fists and allowed her anger to surface. She hated him more than Emily had.

"You," Little Edmond answered. "I've waited long enough. Apparently you aren't coming on your own so I'm simply going to take you with me."

He was so close, too close.

"Don't come one step closer," she said. "I'm warning you."

"Look at you," he said. "Suddenly all brave. What are you

going to do to stop me, Emily?"

"I swear I will kill you," Sarah said. "If I don't, I will beg Farrell to do it for me."

Her mind was running too fast and she couldn't keep up, she was getting dizzy and she knew she was going to faint. Everything started spinning. All she could hear was Little Edmond's laughter. Suddenly, he had her in his grip and she cried out as his fingers bit into her arm and she realized that these were the prints she had seen earlier on her arm.

When Little Edmond pulled her down into the grass, she kicked at him with all of her strength. And then she was on her feet, running as fast as she could, while behind her, he gave chase, his curses filling the air.

Pushing through the trees, a branch caught her arm but she ignored the pain. She didn't have to think anymore. She knew what she was doing, where she was going. She knew she was racing the devil and any minute now she'd come bursting through the cover of the woods and into the open cemetery. From there she would pray to God that she could make it to the other side before he caught her. If she could just make it to the sheriff's house then Emily would not die after all.

Chapter 37

"Emily!" A voice screamed into the night.

Sarah realized she was the one screaming. Somehow, some way, she was outside of Emily's body, able to watch now, nothing more than a speck of existence trapped in the past. Time had fled past and now it was almost dawn.

As Emily broke free of the trees, the sun completed its climb and shone brightly upon the cemetery. Its golden warmth fell across the flat land until it hit the monument, igniting all the tiny fragments of diamond-like sparkle, setting it afire with blue and white light.

In the instant that Sarah was struck by the monument's beauty, the sun reflected off of something metal, creating an intense flash of light and she was forced to throw up her arms to shield her eyes. That was when she saw that Emily was in front of her, approaching the monument. Suddenly, an ear-piercing scream filled the morning silence. Birds flew up out of the trees with raucous cries.

Sarah sprinted across time and space, pumping her arms as hard as she could. Her legs stretched to their limits as each stride took her closer and closer to the monument where she skidded to a stop. But there was nothing there. No Emily, no blood, nothing. Grass swayed in the breeze at the base of the monument.

"Where are you?" Sarah cried out.

All the blood in her body felt as if it was rushing upwards, flooding her brain and she seemed to plummeted backward, drifting away from the cemetery and its headstones until she was surrounded by nothing but trees. And then she was standing in the yard with blue skies above and all of summer buzzing around her. This, too, sped in a sickening motion as she continued to move back. When at last her trip ceased, she was standing in the front room of Emily's house, her back against the door. The door opened and shut with a teeth-shattering slam.

"Emily!" she heard Farrell bark. "Emily, you witch, you liar!"

Sarah felt her body yank backwards. Now she was inside Farrell, feeling and seeing everything he had that fateful day. She could feel the weight of his body as he moved, see through his eyes as he bent over and picked up a crumpled man's shirt from the floor.

She now understood why Farrell was such an angry ghost.

His final rage was not one of hatred. He was clearly terrified of what was happening. Though he roared and carried on like a maniacal bull, she could feel him trembling, she could sense the bitter taste of disbelief and dread that haunted him.

Farrell threw open the back door hard, banging it into the wall, splintering the wood.

"Emily, where are you?" he called out. "Don't play games with me."

Sarah felt herself thrust violently out of Farrell's body as he disappeared into the trees. Running after him, she slid to a stop as Little Edmond came up before her, wicked eyes gleaming.

"Where is she?" Farrell demanded.

"She's mine now," Little Edmond said. "Forever."

"I will kill you if you've hurt her," Farrell growled.

"Will you," Edmond scoffed, leaning against a tree, making a deliberate show of his careless disregard for anything except himself. "I doubt that. The one thing my father taught me that was of any value was how to be a fighter. How to defend myself against scum like you. You don't frighten me, Farrell."

Sarah looked to her left. Sure enough the massive oak tree stood next to Farrell. She knew that this was the end for Farrell. That tree was the spiritual tomb for him.

"I will only ask you once more," Farrell roared. "Where is Emily?"

"Gone. You're stupidity rubbed off on her. She didn't know what was good for her. She thought she could outrun me. But it was thrilling to watch her. There is something immensely sexual about an upset woman, particularly if she is terrified. And Emily *was* terrified. She-"

For all his massiveness, Farrell was swift. His fist smashed Edmond's nose and he followed that with a blow to the face that ripped open a wide gash across his cheek. Without warning, Edmond had armed himself with a baseball bat he had apparently kept hidden behind the massive oak tree.

For the second time, Sarah watched Farrell fall to his death as Edmond struck him over and over again until his face was nothing but a bloody mask. When it was over, Edmond wiped the flowing blood from his face and threw the bat as hard as he could into the thickest part of the woods and disappeared into the shadows.

Farrell wasn't dead yet, though. Falling to her knees, Sarah sat beside him while he struggled to catch what she knew were his last few breaths.

Chapter 38

Sarah awoke with a start. Throwing a pillow over her face, she sobbed. Drenching the pillow with her tears, she cried until all the tears had dried up and all she could do was cough and choke.

Finally, picking up the phone, she dialed Jamie's number.

"Hello?" a sleepy voiced answered.

"Come over quick," Sarah said, as soon as she had hung up, she began to cry again.

After two hours of waiting until every one got there, Sarah finally had her chance to tell them the truth.

"So it *was* Little Edmond," Shane said, leaning back in his chair, letting the back legs balance under his weight.

They were sitting around the kitchen table. Sarah tried to eat the scrambled eggs that Jamie made, but she had no appetite. She knew that her eyes must be red and puffy, and she hadn't even bothered to comb her hair. Not that it mattered at the moment.

"He was only a kid," Dennis said, catching a drip of ketchup from his chin and licking it off his finger before driving his fork into his pile of ketchup-smothered eggs.

"That's really gross," Kate said, making a face.

"Ketchup enhances the flavor of everything," he said.

It was good, Sarah found, to have this period of normality. She knew that they wanted to hear what she had to tell them, and God knows she wanted to tell it, but they were trying hard to play down the drama of what happened to her since Shane hypnotized her, and now this. She appreciated their thoughtfulness.

"As soon as Emily revealed Edmond's involvement, I was suspicious," she told them. "But my god! He was merciless."

"You look like a train wreck, by the way," Todd said. "That must have been some trip."

Todd stood near the kitchen door, tossing a wooden baseball bat back and forth between his hands.

"Where'd you get that?" Sarah demanded.

"By the back door," Todd said. "Why?"

Sarah's tongue was glued to the roof of her mouth.

"Sarah, what's the matter? You look like you've never seen that bat before," Jamie said. "It's just your father's bat."

"She's going to pass out!" Shane jumped out of his chair and caught Sarah just before she fell to the floor.

"I always leave it beside my bed," Sarah said in a low voice. "For protection when my mother isn't here. What is it doing down here?"

"Here drink some orange juice," Jamie said, offering her a small glass.

"Are you okay?" Kate asked, coming to kneel beside her.

"Hey, if you're accusing me of sneaking into your room and stealing your bat..." Todd began.

"I'm not accusing you of anything. I just don't understand how it got in the kitchen," Sarah said drinking the juice and finding that it did, indeed, make her feel better.

"Why does it matter?" Dennis asked.

"Todd, you're a baseball fanatic. How old do you think that bat is?" Sarah asked.

"I'd say it's a vintage. It's old, but it's been taken care of superbly," Todd answered.

"Well," Sarah said, "my dad was always a stickler for keeping things in perfect condition. I know this is going to sound crazy, but Little Edmond killed Farrell with a bat. *That bat*."

Dennis groaned. Todd dropped the bat, which hit the floor with a thud and rolled towards Sarah. At the same time, the temperature dropped so low that their breath plumed out in front of their faces.

"I think someone agrees," Todd said.

A large black shape drifted through the kitchen and disappeared. Immediately it became warm again.

"Okay," Dennis said. "You live in their house, you have Emily's diary and now the very bat that killed Farrell was your father's? How is that possible?"

"Let's not forget that Sarah is Emily's cousin," Todd added. "Way down the line, that is."

Sarah shrugged her shoulders. There were so many pieces to the puzzle, she wasn't sure she could fit them all together. Maybe some of them were not important, like how she and her mother had happened to choose this particular house to live in. But that didn't matter. All they needed to do was put the right puzzle pieces together so that they could put Emily and Farrell to rest.

"If I remember correctly, my dad found it when he was a little boy," she said. "He was visiting family and was playing out in the woods when -" Sarah stopped.

"Woods?" Todd asked.

"Where's your father from?" Dennis asked.

Sarah thought for a moment.

"Originally, he came from here," she said. "Since we lived up north all my life I have never thought about the fact that we moved to his home town."

"Oh this gets better by the minute!" Dennis said.

"We know who killed them," Jamie said. "We have the diary and the bat. Maybe if we just bury them both it will release their spirits from being trapped here."

Sarah looked at the bat still lying on the floor. It had been her protector, her little piece of fatherliness. In a way, it was all she had left of him. Even though he had betrayed her and Mom, she clung to that bat with the hope he might one day come back. If she got rid of the bat, would she be losing him completely? And if she did, did it really matter? Because she knew that he was never coming back. She also knew that she'd be all right without him, she had Emily's strength now.

"We can bury them at the base of the oak tree," she said.

Chapter 39

A big part of her didn't want to let it all go.

As she watched the boys dig a large hole at the base of the oak tree, she held tight to the bat and looked up into the canopy of crisp green leaves. The sun drizzled down keeping most of the darkness at bay. She looked to her left.

Farrell stood there, watching her.

His face was somber, as he remained motionless. As for Sarah, she couldn't move. She just stood there, staring at him.

"Sarah. Earth to Sarah!" Todd called out from within the hole.

She could scarcely hear him over the sound of wind that

drove its way through her head. Sarah could see that Farrell's lips were moving.

"What?" she called to him. "I can't hear you, Farrell. What are you saying?"

The Specters all turned to her with open mouths. Todd began to say something but Shane pinched him.

"Shh, she's connected," he hissed. "Don't interrupt her."

They listened transfixed as Sarah tried again to understand what Farrell was saying.

"I don't see him," Jamie whispered, her eyes following Sarah's.

"He doesn't want us to see him," Shane said. "This is a personal moment."

"Okay. I know. I will," Sarah was saying.

All the sunlight that filtered through the trees seemed to gather within her tears as she turned towards her friends.

"He said, 'Thank You' for doing this," she said, fighting back her tears. "He also said that he understands about my father. How does he know that?"

"That's one of the mysteries of the dead," Shane said. "They seem to know more than can be explained."

Todd climbed out of the hole, dusting the thick dirt from his jean shorts.

"Aw, great. They're stained!" he grumbled.

Dennis and Shane followed, raising themselves up out of the ground. Sarah had the image of them rising from the grave, dead but undead. A shiver stole over her.

"I guess it's time to lay them to rest," Shane said, holding

2ortffortng2rt1

out his hand for the diary and bat.

"I'll do it," Sarah said.

Jamie and Kate quickly readied their cameras and as Sarah knelt before the hole, she heard them click shot after shot. She emptied her mind as she said a silent prayer over the open ground.

"Dad, you left me," Sarah said, dropping the bat into its grave. "Now for the greater good of two lost souls, I have to let you go."

Clutching the diary close to her, she realized that letting it go would be far more difficult. It was her only connection to Emily, her doorway into Emily's life. She was going to lose Emily forever once she buried it.

"It's okay," Shane whispered in her ear and she realized that his arm was around her waist.

"I know," she said. "But I'm going to miss her."

"We all are," he said. "But she needs to rest."

With a sigh, Sarah let the diary fall from her hands.

"Good-bye Emily," she whispered. "May you and Farrell both find peace."

The wind she had previously heard inside her head now hit the woods with such force that a downpour of oak leaves assaulted them, together with the sound of a man's voice and a sorrowful weeping, which rose to a wail, matched that of the wind, and then fell silent as the last leaf fell into the grave.

As the boys shoveled dirt into the hole, Sarah wept, crying for the two lost souls she had come to know so intimately. She wept for her father and for herself. And she saw that Shane was crying, too, as well as Jamie and Kate. Even Todd had to wipe a stray tear from his eye.

Then the raw earth was coated in windblown leaves. And it was over.

Chapter 40

It's been two weeks since we buried the diary, during which I have had no dreams or sightings of Emily or Farrell. I guess that means they are now truly at rest. Strangely enough, both cameras developed nothing but blank film. Some were pitch black while others were a grayish white. But there was not a single image on any of them. Two rolls of film and not a single picture.

Hearing something outside, Sarah stopped writing. It sounded as though something was stepping on branches.

Sarah put her pen down beside her new journal and watched, her stomach knotted with fear as someone stepped out of the woods. Summoning up all her courage, she got up from the table. Very slowly and very carefully, she opened the door and stepped outside.

"Sheriff?" she called out.

"Look," Mr. Brewler said. "I'm sorry to bother you, but you've been haunting me lately."

"Mr. Brewler," Sarah said, relieved.

"May I speak with you?" he said, coming toward her. Now that she could see him clearly, she saw how much he resembled his grandfather.

The similarity was striking. For a moment, Sarah drifted back through time and envisioned Sheriff Brewler holding Emily close, his bright eyes shining. A small sigh escaped her lips.

"Of course," Sarah said. "Come in."

It felt strange to have a living Brewler in her house. She wondered if Emily and Farrell were still there, how would they react? Would they have recognized him? She waited for any sign of paranormal activity, but the house was silent.

"I know it's been awhile since we've last met," he said taking a seat at the kitchen table, facing the back door. "For some reason I haven't been able to sleep. It hasn't bothered me before, not once since that day you kids showed up on my doorstep. But all of a sudden, I can't think, I can't sleep. I haven't even been able to eat much." Mr. Brewler ran a hand through his thinning silver hair.

Again, Sarah was taken aback and saw the Sheriff sitting across from her. Then a thought occurred.

"How did you know where I lived?" Sarah asked, eyeing him with suspicion.

"Ha! Now, that's funny, isn't it? I'll tell you, my father used to take me to that cemetery back there when I was little. He never said why. Never said anything the whole time. Just walked me through it, down that little path through the woods and then he'd just stand and look at this house. It's been empty for a good many years. I took a guess and decided to see if the house was still empty. As I said, I haven't been able to sleep much. Ghosts have been waking me up at night, you know? It's made me start thinking about the past. Listen, there's no point in me beating around the bush. What I want to know is, did you figure it out?"

"Figure what out?" Sarah asked, although she knew. But she wanted him to open up the subject.

"The mystery," he said. "You know, who killed that unfortunate girl."

Sarah swallowed hard. How was she going to tell him that it was his own father? He already suspected his grandfather had something to do with it. But his father? Should she be the one to tell him? After all this time?

"Don't lie to me, Missy," he said as she started to speak. "I can see it in your eyes. Tell me the truth. It was Pops, wasn't it?"

Sarah took a deep breath.

"No, it wasn't," she said. "Your grandfather loved Emily very much but he never would have hurt her. In fact, he tried to protect her when he thought she was being hurt."

He didn't ask her how she knew any of this. Sarah thought she saw denial shade his eyes as he turned to go.

"You're not going to ask who did it?" she said.

"Would you tell me, honestly?"

"Of course," she said. "But only if you asked me to."

"I'll tell you a little secret then," he said, leaning against the doorjamb in just the same way she had once seen his father stand. But there was no mischief or malice in his eyes. They were as kind and sincere as his grandfather's.

"Pops always seemed to resent my dad. It took me until I was a teenager to see it. But once I did, it baffled me. He'd turn on him in a second, sometimes for no reason at all. And then, when Pops was dying, he pulled me aside. He tried to tell me something about being true in the heart and not letting the devil into it. I didn't understand because he'd never been a religious kind of man. And suddenly, all this talk of the devil. Then, when you came to talk to me, it was as though I could see it all - past, present and future. I want to thank you for opening my eyes, even though it hurts."

"I'm really sorry," Sarah said softly.

"I needed to hear it from you, though," he said. "You look just like her."

"I'm a relative," Sarah said. "Believe it or not."

"Figured as much," Mr. Brewler said, his startling blue eyes fixed on her. "That's not what I needed to hear."

Closing her eyes so she didn't have to see his face, she counted to ten. "It was Little Edmond," Sarah said, but Mr. Brewler was already walking away. On the edge of the woods, he turned, looking once more so much like his grandfather that it took her breath away. And then he waved and was gone.

Epilogue

Sarah pushed the last of the boxes into the moving van. She couldn't believe it. All this time had passed and she never even realized her mother was planning on moving into a bigger house. It explained why she had worked so hard during these past several months.

At first Sarah hadn't wanted to move and had tried her best to argue her mother out of it. But with no luck.

"You need to be closer to school and your friends," her mother said. "You're so locked away out here. Besides, I've met a friend, and I'd like to be closer to him."

Her mom had a friend! The world seemed to be moving in hyper drive. She had lost an entire summer, most of last year, in fact. Now that school had begun, Shane already had their next ghost hunt in the making. And she was moving into a bigger house in town.

Yesterday Sarah had ventured off into the woods to visit the little grave by the oak tree. She knelt down and placed a hand on the bare earth. A flicker of white caught her eye. She looked up. Winding its way up the massive trunk, a thin vine snaked along the bark. Tiny white blossoms dotted the vine. Their velvety petals captured the sunlight and glowed.

She still hadn't seen or heard anything of the two. She continued to write down as much as she could in her own journal, recapturing as many of Emily's own words as she remembered. Emily would never be forgotten and Sarah hoped to write a book about Emily and what her life must have been like.

Sarah rolled down the door and latched it. This was it. She was leaving the house. Everything that had tied her to Emily was going to be nothing more than a memory. It was for the best, she guessed. Hopefully the next family to move into this tiny house would not disturb the spirits sleeping within.

As Sarah made her way around the van, a sudden urge to look back halted her steps. She turned, looking over her shoulder. Her mom came out of the house, beaming a bright smile, her purse swinging from her arm.

"Ready?" she asked as she hopped up into the driver's seat.

"I guess so," Sarah answered.

She gave the house a final glance. There in the window, watching her, stood Farrell and Emily, arm in arm.

The End

www.ingramcontent.com/pod-product-compliance
Lightning Source LLC
Chambersburg PA
CBHW020412180626
46812CB00003B/938